Pine Valley Series : Book Three

A PLACE

CALLED

THE WAY

CORRINE ARDOIN

Black Rose Writing | Texas

ISBN: 978-1-68433-995-2
PUBLISHED BY BLACK ROSE WRITING
www.blackrosewriting.com

Printed in the United States of America
Suggested Retail Price (SRP) $19.95

A Place Called The Way is printed in Garamond

Praise for

A PLACE
CALLED
THE WAY

"...a soothing look at how people can share their goodness with others."

—US Review of Books

"This novel highlights relationships and community while giving light emphasis on how culture changes with events and time, but more importantly, highlights how the characters themselves change."

—Pacific Book Review

"*A Place Called the Way* is a multi-generational study and examination of humanity in all its glory and frailty, bringing to mind classics like *The Joy Luck Club* and *One Hundred Years of Solitude.*

—Book Review Directory

"Readers need this story of promise and spiritual growth, and libraries need to not only include it in literary fiction collections about small-town roots, but should point book clubs and discussion groups to its evocative blend of spiritual and social inspection."

—D. Donovan, Sr. Reviewer, *Midwest Book Review*

"*A Place Called The Way* is subtle, intriguing, and filled with hope."

—Independent Book Review

I dedicate this book to my grandchildren,
who bring hope and delight
with each of their beautiful smiles.

SPECIAL THANKS

I would like to give a special thanks to my family for their generous support and for being such good listeners. And, I would like to take this opportunity to acknowledge and give thanks to all my readers. Also, my deepest appreciation and thanks to Reagan Rothe and all the good people at Black Rose Writing. You are *awesome!*

Pine Valley Families

Harrison Stewart (Harry) and Phoebe Adano came to Pine Valley to start a newspaper. Their son, Tucker Howard Stewart, married Adelaide Jones (Addie) and had eight children: June, Howard, Dewey, Henry, Ted, Marjorie, Lois, and Tucker James (Jim). Howard married Mary Weatherby.

Thomas McGrew and son, Ulysses (Uly), were Pine Valley pioneers who ran the store. Ulysses' children were Sam and Clarence (Daddy). Sam's son was Thomas Ulysses (Tommy). Clarence married Patience Walker and had one child: Dorothy Ann (Dottie).

Cedric Cadwallader and sons, William (Bill) and Joseph (Joe), were Pine Valley pioneers who ran the post office. Joseph's sons were Robert (Bobby, Caddie), Geoffrey, and Joseph Reginald. Robert married Charity Walker and had one child: Sylvia, who married Fortuitous Sumner (Forty). Geoffrey's son was Harvey.

Josiah Hart and Rebecca Henry met and married in Pine Valley. Their son, Timothy (Tim), married Alice Smith and helped to run the way station, blacksmith shop, and livery stable. Their children were Jackson, Jimmy (Big Jimmy), and Jefferson. Jimmy married Candelaria Mendoza and had four children: Rosa (Rosalita), James Henry (Little Jimmy, Jim), Joseph, and Baby Hart. Rosa married Stephen Bertram Smith (Buster). James Henry married Bethany Clark (Beth).

Henry Henry and Henrietta Peabody were Pine Valley pioneers who established a way station, blacksmith shop, and livery stable, calling it The Way. Their children were Walter (Walt) and Lulabelle (Sister Ruth). Walter and Lulabelle adopted Johnny. Walter married Millicent May Forester (Millie). Rebecca Henry was Henry Henry's sister.

Jebediah Walker and sons, Joseph and Jiminy Russell, were Pine Valley pioneers who planted the fruit orchards. Jiminy married Charlotte Lee

Caruthers (Char Lee Rosebud) and had four children: Justice, Prosperous (Russ), Patience (Patty), and Charity.

Timoteo Garcia and Josefa Candelaria Bustamante dreamed of going to Pine Valley, but were killed, along with their sons, Jose Timoteo de Jesus and his brother. Their daughter, Maria Estefana (Mama Stefa, Little Fawn), married Joaquin Muscio (Quino). They were Pine Valley pioneers. Their daughter was Maria Evangelica Theresa (Ev).

Berto Mendoza, a ranch hand and miner, married a Pine Valley native, Lucy Shoseegan, and had three children: Jesse, Hermenegildo (Herman), and Manuel (Manny). Jesse married Ev Garcia and had four children: Joaquin, Dexter, Hermenegilda (Gilda), and Candelaria (Laria, Larie). Manuel's son was Aurelio (Leo). Aurelio's daughter was Aurelia (Ellie).

Hector Shoseegan was a Pine Valley native. His children were Dexter Shows-His-Guns and Lucy (Choocha).

Bartholomew Jones (Bart) was a Pine Valley pioneer whose homestead provided the land for Edenville. His daughter was Adelaide (Addie).

Jorge Gutierrez (George) and Esther Chavez (Chavie) were farmworkers. Their daughter was Socorro Alvarez (Coco).

Trudy Price owned Teapot full o' Whimsy. Her daughter, Eileen Price, worked as a nurse and helped at the tea shop.

A PLACE

CALLED

THE WAY

PROLOGUE

Berto Mendoza sat before his humble shack overlooking the valley. He loved his home and fussed over it like a nesting bird. His wife, Lucy, his darling Choocha, was up the hill with the brother and sister, Walter Henry and Lulabelle. They were orphans since their father was killed and their mother died. So sad, Berto thought, wondering why they had to suffer. Tears pooled in his eyes, his heart filling with love for all humanity, even those who were greedy, for he knew they suffered most of all, in their ignorance.

Ideas and poems filled the journal he held in his lap, but the words did not come easy. The blank page stared at him, waiting. He heard people gathering for the first picnic in Pine Way. His eldest son, their last to leave home, was going to announce his marriage at the picnic. Afterward, his son planned to live in the new home he had built for his wife. Berto and Lucy would be alone in their little shack for the first time in many years.

Berto returned to his journal, deciding to write a poem about life.

"I'll call it, 'The Mysterious Journey,' because life is a mystery," he said.

Speaking the words aloud as he wrote, he said, "Life has so much to offer a man. Yet, he comes up against so many who claim, 'No, you cannot do this. You cannot go there.' Why is so much shown to those who can achieve so little?" The answer came to him as it was being written, his pain expressed so clearly on the page as he read, "While those who have so much, give waste to the days thus taken from those who strive to walk the Way?"

He was surprised at what he had written. The Way? What is that? What did Henry Henry mean? Walter Henry and Lulabelle's father gave his life defending it. Berto remembered hearing about it in his youth, his abuela's words, his grandmother reading to him from a book she held dear. She wore a scarf wrapped over her head and her voice was but a whisper. When she was done reading, she kissed her book and sat in silence. He could not remember the entire passage which she had read, but he knew, at least he thought he knew...the Way.

CHAPTER ONE

A light breeze blew tattered bits of hay gently swirling and dancing upon the wind. The brown-haired boy swept his hands together, looking on at what he could do, what his small fists could grasp and throw. Drying tears left their salty crust upon his face, but the memory, ugly and raw, lingered in his young heart. He looked down at the dirt where he stood and saw ants he had riled. Stomping his cowboy boots as much as his four-year-old feet could, he smashed them before they scurried onto his boots.

The boy's mother hurried out of the barn and scooped him up, kicking and screaming.

"Let me down!" he said.

"Let's get you home, Jimmy," she said in a fearful tone. "I want to get out of here before Mean Uncle returns."

She held him close. He quieted and allowed her to carry him, between the trees, following the path across the field, to their home on the other side.

A thin and wiry woman, named Candelaria Hart, she cast quick glances behind her and around the field, needing to be sure they went unseen. Her daughter, Rosalita, had run homeward first sight of Uncle Jackson riding down the dirt road astride his slipshod mare.

He had come to ask his brother to take care of his horse while he went "somewhere." With Uncle Jackson, asking was the same as telling. He was a bully in the way others regarded his stern ways, though in his own mind, he was only doing what he believed was the best way. After all, he was the eldest, and his way, Uncle Jackson's way, was the right way, the only right way.

Slumped to the right in his saddle as though having ridden a hundred miles, one would have assumed he was drunk. His beaten-up hat, flopping and torn, rested lopsided on his head. Well, he was drunk, but he always sat that way out of "pure cussedness," according to Walter Henry, who heard Rosalita's warning.

"Here comes Mean Uncle!"

She ran home, her long braids flapping and swinging in her swiftness. Looking at the ground ahead of her as she scurried off like a startled rabbit, she made her way along the path.

Candelaria shouted to her. "Rosalita!" she said. "Wait!" She wanted to be sure it was safe to go home.

When they arrived, she saw no one around. She had hoped her husband would be there, but he was not. She set her son down in the living room. He ran off to hide under his bed, his tiny boots clunking on the wood flooring until he dragged himself into the shadows like a wounded dog.

Candelaria hid her worried face with her hand, catching her tears. Overwrought and shaken, she entered the children's bedroom and pulled her son out from under the bed. She saw red marks on his skin and a knot on his forehead. A long cut down the inner length of his left forearm was bandaged in a hurry back at the barn. She held him close to her and sat on the bed.

While rocking him, she gave him tender kisses on his forehead. He went limp in her arms. This time, she let herself cry without reservation. She knew Walter Henry would tell her husband. She was sure of it. The thought also came to her that Uncle Jackson might get—

Candelaria felt too tired to think about what might happen. Rosalita sat on the bed beside her and leaned against her. She kissed her daughter's head and knew that the old family story had come to life once more.

•   •   •

Late one night, listeners gathered in the barn to hear the tale. They seated themselves on barrels and bales of hay. Grieved expressions appeared haunted by the flickering light of the lantern as Walter Henry shared what he knew about Josiah Hart.

Josiah arrived in town, trailing behind a small group of travelers. Walter Henry's father, Henry Henry, spoke with the travelers at the way station, only a few families, men and their wives, with several children. They were suspicious of the rough-looking and unkempt man who had followed them. Not wanting any trouble, they said, they welcomed him at their nightly campfires on the trail. They were eager to part company with the man.

When the travelers were ready to continue on, Josiah Hart nodded to them, a nod that meant, "thank you," "goodbye," and "you're good people," all at the same time. Relieved, they left the way station, while he remained.

People traveling the road to the way station were greeted by a sign that read, "Welcome to The Way." However, the rangy, wild-looking Josiah Hart was welcomed solely by one person, a short, hard-working, and wide-hipped woman claimed by spinsterhood at thirty-two. Not exactly a homely woman, she had her eye on every available bachelor, all three of them. But, they would not have her. Too tough, too independent-minded for them, and too "broad in the beam," were their words. Humiliated and long ago having given up on marriage, Josiah Hart's hungry eyes on her frame both terrified and, surprisingly, excited her. He had her won with that look and she soon had him wrangled with her cooking.

Her name was Rebecca Henry, the way station owner's sister and the cook. She knew, like no one else, how to melt men's hearts, if not having won her any marriage proposals in the past. To put it another way, she had the means to get to their stomachs, but not their arms. Josiah welcomed both and lifted the hefty woman off the station's porch where she stood in silent awe of her husband-to-be. He set her down, still grasping her shoulders and looking into her eyes. She held his gaze like no other.

Children appeared regularly as though baked in an oven, like loaves of bread, every two years until there were five, one son, the eldest, and four daughters. Josiah had built his wife a cabin on the outskirts of Pine Valley, where one could see for themselves the changes being wrought with each tree that fell. Only a small grove remained. It was on land granted to a local tribe of natives. The few tribal members who lived there had no immediate plans to leave. Their bark houses once dotted the entire valley floor where cool breezes and berry thickets were best, all summer long. Their aging patriarch, Hector Shoseegan, kept an eye on the town's lone ruffian ever since his arrival.

Rebecca fell ill from an unknown sickness that grew worse over the years. She tried to keep up the cooking for the way station, but it killed her. She died from sheer exhaustion at the sunset of her forties. The way station owner had his wife take over the cooking, like she had done in the beginning when they first came to the valley. Their maid and her daughter managed all the housekeeping.

Josiah's son, Timothy, had apprenticed with Henry Henry as a blacksmith, starting when he was twelve. Big for his age, he was soon able to handle even large draft horses and mules. He was respected and well-liked by the way station's proprietors, his Aunt and Uncle Henry. Josiah, on the other hand, was never the same after the death of his wife. It was decided that his four daughters should be sent away to live with family elsewhere. With their brother managing the team, they climbed aboard the wagon and departed, leaving their father a changed man. He turned old overnight. Not only had he reached the end of his day, but he had reached the end of the road. Why he chose not to go with his children was an unfortunate decision. His grief, everyone could see for themselves, was taking its toll.

Timothy understood he was to return home to his father, but he postponed the trip until after a year had passed. He was seventeen and bringing his new bride home to meet the rest of the family.

Weeks before he finally decided to come home, his father, bereft and taken to drink, shot and killed Timothy's uncle during an argument that began over the town's unusual name. They were standing in the road between the way station and the livery stable. People could hear the quarrel grow louder. Josiah, his long, curly hair grayed, his face and very form haggard and thin, clothes filthy, stood there staggering, wanting to fight.

He said, "Nobody's gonna respect a town called, 'The Way.' What kind of a name is that, anyway?"

"To be thankful to the Lord, by gawd! He is my Shepherd and I shall not want!" answered Henry Henry in defense of his town's beloved appellation. "That's why I call it The Way! So, I don't want to hear another word about it!" he said.

Many a tale related how he walked away from Josiah to begin work for the day at the blacksmith shop. Unwilling to let the matter rest, he turned around and criticized Josiah for daring to come into his town that day long ago, wearing a Confederate uniform.

"Probably rode with the guerrillas!" He flung his arm out there somewhere. "That's what you are, nothing but a big gorilla!"

Josiah's mood darkened, his eyes revealing stark, penetrating cruelty. He said, "Yeah, I rode with them and, let me tell you, I'm damned proud of it!" He poked his finger at Henry Henry to drive home his point. "Never should've ended slavery!" he said.

This unexpected outburst further riled the blacksmith. His curly, thinning, and graying brown hair became bushy and wispy all at once, like an upset, old, frazzled tomcat. With mustache twitching, he determined to say the final word.

"Slavery was an abomination on this country's very soul!" he said, throwing his arm in a wide arc as if to sweep across the land, thus adding dramatic effect to his passionate analogy. Adding with equal passion, with right arm raised and index finger aiming heavenward, he pontificated, "President Lincoln was the saint of this bless-ed nation to put an end to it!"

Josiah turned for the worse, saying with a sneer, "Lincoln?" He spat on the ground, then sunk lower. "Well, Mr. Lincoln-lover," he said, "wouldn't he like to know you've got yourself a couple of mighty convenient, Mexican slave women cleanin' your house!"

Henry Henry mumbled as he hurried back to the station, "I'm gonna get my gun and make that man leave this town, like I should've done from the start!"

Josiah leered at him as he said, "Don't waste your time," and fired a shot. Whether he had aimed to kill or merely to startle his opponent, Henry Henry dropped.

Hector Shoseegan, hovering in the vicinity during their argument, pulled his own gun out of its holster and shot Josiah dead. He heard from behind, the young Walter Henry shouting to his slain father, "Papa!" Wheeling around to grab the boy and hold on to him, Hector kept Walter Henry from looking at his father lying dead beside his enemy.

Henrietta Henry screamed, raising a vehement appeal to the heavens, having witnessed Josiah murder her husband. Hector walked the boy over to her. She drew her son down to kneel beside her and they cried in each other's arms.

Hector disappeared. Aside from his daughter, Lucy, the Shoseegan's and the remainder of their tribe fled into the mountains. They needed to protect Hector from getting hunted down and killed. But, no one went to look for him. The townspeople were secretly thankful and spoke not a word about his involvement in the incident. They prayed for peace to return to their valley.

Not long after the tragedy, Timothy returned with his new bride. He helped his wife get down from the wagon when Walter Henry stepped outside the barn. He looked as sad as a wounded bird, holding the fingers of both his hands together like a frightened child. Great sadness showed in his eyes and upon his face. An ominous feeling came over Timothy when he dared to ask the boy what was wrong.

"My papa's dead, Tim," said Walter Henry.

"Dead?" Timothy asked, not understanding. "How? When?"

The storekeeper, Thomas McGrew, called Timothy over to the store and told him what had happened. Crying in the man's arms, Timothy realized he was yet a boy, himself. Fear struck his heart at the loss of his father and his uncle. Not knowing what else to do, he and Walter Henry continued working like they always had before their fathers were killed.

The two young men ran the blacksmith shop and the livery stable on their own. Timothy's wife, Alice, helped with the cooking at the way station. They began a family and her parents moved there and built the house Candelaria and her husband would live in one day.

It was Timothy and Alice who had Jackson, their first-born child. Their second child was Jimmy, after whom his own son was named. Jefferson was the youngest, but Jackson, who became "Mean Uncle," would outlive them all. It was he who left his jagged mark upon the soul of his nephew, Little Jimmy Hart.

CHAPTER TWO

Candelaria knew the history of the family into which she had married. Her husband's grandfather was killed after he shot his own brother-in-law. For the two families to be in business together seemed strange to her, but unless she talked about it to find out why, she would never know the answer. How Jackson Hart got to be so mean, she never knew, but then he left town.

Holding her son close to her, she rocked him gently. "There, there," she said. Well, Jackson may have gone away, she thought, but her son's nightmares kept the man very present in their lives.

Her husband, Big Jimmy, looked in the unlit bedroom and asked, "Why are you babying that boy?"

Two years had gone by and, once more, she sat in the dark on the edge of the bed. The light from the living room slanted in and she looked up at her husband, standing there in all his glory, she noted, the hat, the boots, the jeans.

"He had a nightmare again," she explained. She hoped the light would not betray her tears.

Big Jimmy stood there tapping the open door with the backs of his fingers. He had worked extra hard that day and wanted to eat dinner and—

"Come on, sweetie pie," he gestured with his head, nodding toward the kitchen to show her he wanted her to "come on."

She laid their son down and covered him. Rosalita stirred on their shared bed, the slant of light growing larger as her husband opened the door wider. It revealed the scar on their son's arm.

Big Jimmy felt the pain of guilt strike him hard in his gut. He turned away and went into the kitchen. Candelaria followed him.

"When's that boy gonna get over it?" He was referring to the incident that left their son scarred.

Candelaria served him his dinner, a plate of frijoles and a chunk of cornbread. She had no patience in making tortillas. She poured him a glass of milk as he got himself a pickled jalapeño and a hot carrot slice from the jar on the table.

"I don't know," she answered. "Maybe Uncle Dexter knows something we can do." He was her great-uncle who lived in the mountains.

She leaned back against the kitchen counter, her apron on and her own cowboy boots and blue jeans dusty and in need of a rest. Her arms were crossed in front of her as she looked down at the linoleum floor, worrying about her son.

Big Jimmy was finished eating. He drank his milk and rubbed his mouth clean with his sleeve. He sat in a chair as if he was mounting a horse and then similarly dismounted. Approaching his wife, he wrapped his arms around her, down low around her hips, so he could pull her close to him as he kissed her on the neck.

He asked, "You know what I think?"

"What?" Candelaria looked up, sadly hopeful for another idea, interested.

"I think you and me better get ourselves a bath and get to bed." He laughed, giving his wife a quick spank. "Let's go!"

Candelaria laughed, sort of, shook her head and begrudgingly went with him, having agreed they both smelled like the corral.

Later that night, she lay awake thinking about her grandmother, Estefana Garcia, who had emotional problems. Angry at God for what happened to her grandmother as a child and for her boy getting so brutally hurt, she wondered how He, so Almighty, could be so cruel as to let children get hurt. She ruminated fearfully, believing that a curse had been laid upon them, not only on the Hart's and the Henry's, but on the Garcia's, too.

When Candelaria was a child, an old man would come to her parent's house. He would bring food or little gifts and stay and visit with them. His name was Joaquin Muscio. Joaquin once worked as a ranch hand, but had become too old to do that anymore. He drove a Model T, tooting the horn when he neared their home. She and her siblings would run up to the car and surround him, hoping for some special treat. "Papa Quino!" they would say. He would give each of them a hug, making sure he scratched their smooth cheeks with his whiskery face and tickled them. They would all laugh.

No one ever talked about it, but Joaquin was her mother's father. He never lived with them. Neither her mother nor her grandmother had taken his name. Candelaria and her siblings called their grandmother, "Mama Stefa."

It was during one of Joaquin's visits when Josiah's name was mentioned. The family was sitting together in the living room.

Candelaria and her siblings were home from school, sitting cross-legged on the rug.

Her brothers were begging Papa Quino, "Tell us the story about Josiah Hart."

Candelaria remembered herself saying, "Tell us, Papa Quino."

Mama Stefa grew frightened, saying repeatedly in Spanish, "A cursed man...a cursed man." She motioned the sign of the cross, blessing herself, and left the room.

Candelaria's mother, Ev, looked at Joaquin with fear and worry in her eyes.

Joaquin took his leave. Stiffly, and with a groaning effort, he got up from the couch. "Well, mi hija. I'd better go now," he said. He patted each child on the head and walked across the room as though his aching back was rebelling to go anywhere.

"No, don't go," begged Candelaria's eldest brother.

Her mother and her siblings followed Joaquin out the door to his car, leaving Candelaria behind in the house. She went to place her arm around Mama Stefa, who was standing with fists clenched, gripping the lace runner draped atop the dresser in her bedroom. Her eyes were squeezed shut and her head turned down as though looking away from some terrible memory. Candelaria believed her grandmother was in great pain.

"I'm sorry, Mama Stefa," she told her grandmother.

CHAPTER THREE

Rosalita played with her dolls in the garden. She knelt on the ground at her favorite spot, where the argument between her mother and father could no longer reach her ears. Her mother had a temper and her father, as was his habit, had become frustrated.

"Damn! Woman!" her father said in anger.

That was when Rosalita hurried outside with her toys.

Big Jimmy failed to notice. He rubbed his unshaven jaw in exasperation and said to his wife, "You got too much fire in you!" Storming out of the house on his way back to work at the livery stable, he continued yelling. Throwing his hands in the air in frustration, he asked, "What are you so angry about?! Would you just tell me that much?!"

No answer, so he kept walking away, muttering and grumbling.

Candelaria remained standing on the front porch, arms crossed in front of her, feeling so helpless. She asked herself why she was so angry, but no answer came to her, either, so she went back to cleaning the kitchen.

Rosalita waited, her dolls carefully arranged in the tall grass, her toy horses lined up and ready to carry them away on an imaginary mission. At the side of the house, a window screen popped out and fell to the ground. Little Jimmy climbed out of the window and dropped down. He immediately ran over to her, kicking her dolls and horses amid Rosalita's shouts for him to stop.

"Jimmy! Stop it! Mom! Jimmy's being bad again!"

She hurriedly gathered her dolls and horses only for Little Jimmy to try knocking them out of her hands.

"Jimmy! Stop! What's the matter with you?!"

Candelaria followed the direction of Rosalita's shouting and swept the boy into her arms. His tiny fists hit her with all their might, his body thrashing and wrestling to be freed.

Rosalita stood in place, watching her mother carry Little Jimmy in his angry tantrum. They sat on the porch steps, her mother holding him on her lap, calming him by rocking back and forth and softly singing a song. Even at age nine, Rosalita knew they were two of a kind. Her mother was not only soothing the boy their uncle had hurt, Rosalita observed, she was also comforting herself.

Rosalita brushed off her dolls and toy wooden horses. Walter Henry hand-carved each horse and crafted their leather bridles and saddles. She loved them. For Little Jimmy, he also made a model of a horse-drawn wagon, pulled by a pair of horses, with a rope and barrels in the wagon bed, even a tiny bale of hay. Their mother stored it at the barn, along with other toys. Rosalita and her brother were playing with them when their uncle arrived. She believed she had made the wrong choice, hiding the toys, then running home. She wished she had instead made sure her brother followed her. Regretting her actions, she knew he would not have gotten hurt, if she had only taken him with her. After that incident, she tried to remember to be extra watchful and protective of her brother.

The wind was picking up and storm clouds rolled overhead. Rain was coming in fast. They needed to get into the house. Rosalita inspected the damage Little Jimmy inflicted upon her dolls and horses. Thankfully, they were all right. Her brother had calmed down, so they went inside. Remaining watchful, Rosalita tried her best not to upset either of them.

Placing her dolls on top of her dresser out of her brother's reach, Rosalita recalled something her Grandma Ev once told her. It was after Little Jimmy had kicked her when they were at their grandparent's house. Crying and rubbing her shin where his cowboy boot struck her, she yelled after him as he ran off to hide. Grandma Ev advised her to "let Grandpa take care of him," and took her hand, bringing her into the house.

Setting fresh-baked oatmeal raisin cookies and a glass of milk on the kitchen table for her, Grandma Ev looked over Rosalita's injuries and gave her prognosis.

"You'll be fine," she said.

Rosalita wiped her tears with her sleeve and asked her grandmother, "Why does he have to be so mean?"

Her grandmother sat looking out the window, one elbow propped on the table, her chin resting in her hand.

Rosalita said, "My daddy said that my mommy has too much anger in her. Is that what's wrong with Little Jimmy, Grandma? Does he have too much anger, too?" She waited, watching her grandmother for a sign she had even been listening.

Grandma Ev then made the mysterious comment while gazing out the window. "They have wild spirits, Rosalita," she said. With a worried look on her face, she added, "I don't know what will become of your brother if he stays so angry."

• • •

Candelaria was born in that house, along with her sister and her two brothers. Her sister died from cancer when she was only nineteen. Her two brothers lived in another town with their own families, visiting on special occasions. They had witnessed Candelaria's anger, and Little Jimmy's, but usually laughed over it, teasing them both. She failed to see the humor in being so overtaken by emotion that she could no longer control herself. This behavior was what she had seen in her son. Though she believed she knew the source of his anger, she had yet to understand her own.

The rain passed, so they returned outdoors. Rosalita and Little Jimmy wanted to go to their grandparent's house. Candelaria went to the livery stable to help their dad and, hopefully, make it up to him for having been so angry earlier.

She kept quiet as she brushed the horses in the barn. Her mind wandered and she thought of her grandfather, Joaquin. She remembered one time when she was a child. She had arrived home from school after an especially trying day coping with ridicule. Still angry about others having ganged up on her on the playground, and not being able to fight them, she planned to tell her parents about it. Mama Stefa was still living at the time and Joaquin was visiting.

He saw the brooding girl walking toward the house with her brothers and her sister, like a black cloud, full of rain and ready to burst out crying. He thought how cute she was with her hair in pigtails and her two front teeth missing. Although, he wondered why she remained outside, holding her school papers and schoolbook close to her chest, tight in her grip while pacing the yard and circling. From inside the house, he watched her as she threw the book and papers on the ground and stomped on them, tearing the papers and grinding the book into the dirt. He hurried outside and picked her up like she was a kitten.

Candelaria became infuriated. Thrashing about in his arms, she tried to scratch and bite him, imagining she was a powerful lion and was fighting to be free. He carried her over to a bench where they sat alone. She was still fuming. Telling her to sing along with him, he began singing a song. Mama Stefa came outside and joined them. She took Candelaria from Joaquin and held her, rocking her as, together, they sang the song. It was a native lullaby originating with the Shoseegan's. They taught it to Mama Stefa when she was a girl, upset by fire or by her memories of loss.

Even though Candelaria learned what she later taught Little Jimmy, she continued to get overly angry, admitting to herself that she was rebelling. Humbled by this admission, she remained silent, still feeling the sting of her husband's words when he left the house. She was roused back to the present by him.

He was getting some things together before delivering the horse she was brushing, and asked, "You still angry, or somethin'?"

"No." But, she was afraid.

"Then, why're you brushin' that horse so rough?"

Candelaria stopped. She looked at the brush in her hand as though it would give her the answer, then looked at Big Jimmy with a worried expression on her face.

"You'll strip the hide clean off its bones!" he warned her, before he burst out laughing.

Candelaria was in a pensive mood, he had observed, still smoldering since their argument earlier at the house. He said, "Come 'ere," and waved her toward him, holding her in his arms. "I'm just teasin' ya, sweetie pie. You know that."

Still no response from her, so he held her away from him and looked into her eyes. He became concerned.

"What's goin' on?" he asked.

She turned away and, not answering, swept his hands from where he held her.

"Larie?" He pronounced her name as though it was "Lottie."

Candelaria looked toward the door at the back of the barn. Her actions bothered Big Jimmy. He sensed she was more than the usual hot bucket of coals, so he waited. He took hold of the reins and led the horse outside, where he could feel less confined by the confrontation at hand, hoping to distract himself and give her some time. The sun was quickly disappearing. Thick clouds had rolled in and it was threatening to rain again. He busied himself with looking over the horse, needlessly checking its eyes and ears while Candelaria sauntered further away from him toward the back entrance of the barn.

She finally answered him. "I'm pregnant," she said to the ground, the air, the walls, but not to his face. Looking up at the beams, she wondered if they might fall from their hold, so she would then be free, excused from the world and all its difficulties.

CHAPTER FOUR

The discovery that she was going to have a baby used to bring Candelaria joy. When Rosalita was born, life was perfect, it seemed to her. They were innocent. They had become a family. They had enough, enough money, enough time, enough love. Then, Little Jimmy came along. It was fine, at first, except he was a boy. Grandpa Hart and all the Hart men took it upon themselves to make sure he would not grow up to be a "ninny," or, worse yet, "a mama's boy," holding on to the apron, or, as Uncle Jackson said, "teat." Jackson's comment had infuriated Candelaria, embarrassing her.

Daily, she was reminded of the horrible incident, when Jackson, the children's "Mean Uncle," pushed her aside. She went to pick up Little Jimmy from the ground where he dumped the boy after roughing him up.

"It's good for him! You don't want this boy to grow up soft, do ya?"

The sneer on his face repulsed Candelaria.

Walter Henry stepped forward and said to Jackson, "We got your horse. We'll take care of it while you're gone. So, why don't you go on now." He pointed his head toward the door, meaning, "git!"

No one told Jackson when to do anything. He grabbed Little Jimmy from Candelaria's arms and prevented her from taking him back, pushing her away, saying, "I'm not through!"

Angry and coarse, he warned Candelaria with his eyes, piercing her heart. She knew he would do anything. Her boy was in jeopardy. She wondered where her husband had gone, noticing Walter Henry left the barn.

Jackson gave Little Jimmy a lesson on how to be a man. The boy began crying, then wildly screaming for him to stop. Jackson was pushing him around, saying hurtful things, knocking him down. The boy was helpless, unable to get away from the man. His mother twice lunged at Jackson, her own cries coming from out of what felt like her wounded, bleeding heart, but he would push her down again.

"You Mexican ladies!" he said. "You always gotta treat your boys like they was some kind of prince! You baby 'em and don't even let 'em get dirty!"

She tried to grab her son away from him, but Jackson would not allow it. He was a big man, a forceful and a cruel man.

Little Jimmy let out a high-pitched scream Candelaria would never be able to erase from her mind until the day she died. Jackson had done something. It happened so fast.

Walter Henry re-entered the barn, cocked his rifle, and aimed it at Jackson. He said, "I told you to git!"

Candelaria rushed to pick up her son from where he lay by the work bench. She hurried to the wash basin behind the barn to clean his arm, hastily bandaging it with a roll of gauze from their first-aid kit. He was still screaming, though it seemed to her he had gone away. His eyes no longer showed who he was, having become vacant, empty of hope, of life, rolling directionless as though awash in waves of pain and sorrow. She held him close to her, afraid to do anything, afraid to leave, afraid to—

After what seemed like an hour, Walter Henry, having followed Jackson out of the barn, came back inside and said, "Jackson's gone."

It sounded serious. Candelaria felt uncertain she or her son were safe.

He instructed her, "You better take him home. I'll let Jimmy know what his brother done." He held on to his rifle and checked outside and down the road again.

Candelaria struggled to recall what had happened, trying to break the spell. Little Jimmy wanted down, so she set him by the doorway. She stood watching him play with the hay, tossing it into the air, reminiscent of when he was a toddler. She had forgotten Rosalita went home. The moment she thought of it, she picked up her son and ran.

. . .

After recalling the awful experience, Candelaria held herself. Learning she was pregnant again terrified her.

The rain began falling loudly and heavily. The roar from it hitting the barn roof further frightened her.

Walter Henry took the lead rope from Big Jimmy's hand. "I can deliver the horse," he said. He loaded it into the horse trailer.

Candelaria told her husband, "No, you go ahead and go." She rushed out of the barn, walking hurriedly back to their house in the rain.

Big Jimmy was beside himself over what to do. "Damn! That woman is—" He was going to say, "a tough one," but Walter Henry interrupted him.

"What do you want to do?" He closed up the horse trailer and, not wanting to stand around in the rain, pressed his partner for a decision, standing there, waiting.

"Oh, you go ahead, Walt." Big Jimmy dreaded what he needed to do, hoping it would end all right. "I need to sort things out with my wife," he said.

Soon, Walter Henry was gone, driving to a highly respected client who paid well. Big Jimmy was disappointed. He wanted to go with him. At the entrance to the barn, he stood as his partner drove away, tires splashing in potholes filling with rain.

Sometimes, Big Jimmy found it impossible to figure things out, especially since his parents moved away and his younger brother went off to war. He wondered what happened to their lives. Too many men had gone, it seemed to him. Being on the forgotten end of town, nevertheless, brought him comfort.

"Old Pine Way," he said.

It was once a good name for a good town, he thought. It appeared to be a dying one since the war started. His neighbors were moving into the newer houses across the valley. Not so new anymore, but the houses in Pine Way were at least fifty years older than the ones built in Edenville. Big Jimmy preferred the Pine Way houses, arguing with anyone who dared complain.

"These houses here have character!" he would say. "Not like those modern homes with their lawns and fake window shutters and asphalt shingles and all that stuff. I like a house that can breathe."

He looked down the road past the brick buildings of Pine Way, feeling as though something was amiss. He thought about how things had changed and about the war, not hearing from his brother in months. He watched shopkeepers closing for the day and he watched the rain fall. He could not help but love it. He wanted his children to grow up there, like he had. But, ever since his parents moved away, nothing was the same, not the town, or the people.

"Hell," he reasoned, "people even think differently."

He recalled someone in the post office once said, "I'm tellin' ya, the whole world's changed."

Nowhere could Big Jimmy find a place untouched by the war, even his work, slowly tapering off until job offers from down in the valley became tempting. He lowered his head, saddened, not knowing what to do.

His grandparents were gone, all dead. After his mother's parents, the Smith's, passed away, his mother got to pining for her own family. So, his father packed them up and brought her back to her people, whom he also missed, Big Jimmy had heard. That was when he and Candelaria got the house, a few years back. He missed his dad. The gap his father's absence left behind was unsettling. Was it right, he asked himself, for a son to be without his dad? What was he to do? He figured their moving away was why his brother, Jefferson, still unmarried, joined the service when he was in his thirties.

Big Jimmy rarely felt the need to cry. Watching the rain come down, watching it pour, then ease up, with the sun shining so bright that it glared, he did cry. He could smell fresh horse dung and sweet alfalfa hay, plus the resinous oils in the bushes and trees by the road, damp with steam rising from them each time the sun shone again. It made him cry. It was profound, the day, somehow. He believed that if he could only hold on to it and bring it to his hurting wife and his poor little boy and his pretty girl, everything would be all right.

"Oh, Daddy!" he cried to his father far away, needing him badly. But, he was not there where he needed him, when Big Jimmy felt small and helpless, his hands not strong enough and his mind...not smart enough.

Hands in his pants pockets to warm them, the reality of his simple life appeared small and inconsequential. He was only a blacksmith, a farrier. It was all he knew. He could take care of horses, the best around for miles, but it seemed like he could not take care of his own family. Stepping further into the barn, he glanced across the interior, seeing the stacks of junk accumulating in one darkening corner, the tack in disarray. Some of it was lying in the dirt. The horses had settled down, thankfully, but the job was never done. No, there was always something that needed doing.

He locked up the place, turned his collar up, and headed down the path for the house, for home, praying as he walked, like he had a reason to hope.

"Anything you got, Lord," he said, "I'm happy to take from you. My family's hurtin' and if you could help us out, I'd be grateful."

By the time he got home, the answer came to him. They would take a trip to visit his parents. He wondered how they would find the money to do it and decided to look into some job offers he was getting from horse breeding and racehorse outfits. That's how he could get the money. First of all, though, he and his wife needed to have some time alone.

CHAPTER FIVE

Up the porch steps he ran, opening the front door and calling to his wife. "Larie!" he said. He closed the door and removed his boots. He took off his hat and wet jacket, glancing across the room before hanging them on the coatrack. Candelaria was in the kitchen, staring into the cupboard, so he acted fast.

"Say, sweetie pie, how about you and me goin' to town?" he asked.

He approached the kitchen and leaned against the frame of the doorway, hands in his pockets, hopeful, but not wanting to get too close to her, yet. Her eyes still held their tears, he noticed, so he hugged her and asked, "Hmm? What d'ya say?" He tried dancing with her. "When was the last time you and me went dancin', huh?"

She smiled and said, "It's been since we married."

"Well, then, let's go!" He spun her around and drew her close to him. "Maybe the kids could stay the night at your folks," he said, grinning.

Candelaria playfully pushed him away. "That's how I got this," she said, sad-like and pouting as she patted her belly, meaning being pregnant.

Big Jimmy was having fun. "Well," he said, "you're already pregnant, so it can't happen twice at the same time, can it?" He laughed and pulled her close to him again.

She play-hit him and shook her head. "You!" she said.

The children were happy to stay the night at Grandma Ev's and Grandpa Jesse's. Big Jimmy and Candelaria, meanwhile, enjoyed themselves at a honky tonk in a nearby town. They had a cheap dinner, some hamburgers, french fries, and sodas. Although, Big Jimmy ordered a beer afterward.

"To settle my nerves before we get out on the dance floor." He winked at her, laughing and grinning.

Candelaria tried her best to relax and have fun. She commented on the looks directed their way.

"Of course! That's because I'm here," he said.

She shot him a look, lightly laughing.

"With the prettiest woman in the whole town," he told her.

He admired how attractive she was in her bright blue-and-white flowered dress, with her thick, dark hair up in a cute ponytail. Reaching across the table, he took her hand and looked into her eyes.

"In the whole world," he said.

The music started and couples assembled on the dance floor. The women in their flared skirts that twirled and swung, gave flashing smiles to their partners. The fiddler was tapping his toe to the beat. His glasses reflected the overhead lighting.

Bright eyes and clip-on earrings, Candelaria noticed. She could almost hear promises made in bobby-pinned hair and a look just-so. This return to their old social life, brought the past into view once more, both exhilarating and terrifying. She had stolen Big Jimmy from a life of bachelorhood that centered around those very promises. Her arrival on the scene, wearing the ring he had given her, caused more than a few women to look at her with disdain. She practically tore him from the arms of one woman in particular, as that woman, herself, phrased it. Candelaria was on the lookout for her.

Big Jimmy could guess what was preventing his wife from having a good time. "Relax," he said, and drained his beer. "You're the only one in this room who matters to me," then added teasingly, "except the band!" He laughed out loud.

Candelaria also laughed. Finishing her soda, she sat tapping one foot to the beat, unable to remain unaffected by the excitement surrounding her.

Big Jimmy took her hand, jerked his head over to the dance floor, and said, "Come on! Let's dance!"

•   •   •

They arrived home late at night. The door was barely closed and car keys set aside before Big Jimmy placed his arms around his wife, and his hands everywhere he could.

Candelaria was enjoying their playfulness. "Just a minute," she told him.

She remembered the lacy, sheer nightgown her mother had made for her as a bridal shower gift, which drew whoops and whistles from the other women that came to the party. Her mother knew what a man enjoyed. Even though Candelaria mostly thought of her mother as her mother, she had seen glimpses growing up, of her parent's own playfulness and love-making, kissing and hugging and squeezing. It brought a smile to her face as she cleaned up in the bathroom and put on the gown, a pastel pink, mere wispy fluff that barely reached her thighs. It never looked this revealing before, she thought. Seeing herself in the mirror, she felt more naked with it on, than when she really was nude. Her belly, she could feel, was growing. More than a few months along, she put off telling Big Jimmy as long as she could. Her mother kept telling her not to wait.

Ev was doing her mending in her favorite chair. She pushed her reading glasses back up on their perch atop her head and urged her daughter, "Laria! Tsk, tsk, tsk. He needs to know!"

Candelaria smiled in remembrance, but told herself to stop thinking about her mother and father, and her children, so she could get in the mood again. No need to worry about that, she soon learned. She stepped out of the bathroom and went into the bedroom. Her husband was awestruck and, like a madman, practically leapt out of bed. No pooching-out belly was on his mind, evidently, nor the few gray strands that dared to appear in her dark brown mass of hair. She smiled demurely. It felt like the first time. She was eighteen again and he was the young man who embraced her when they fell in love.

Big Jimmy was right, he told himself. They needed time alone with one another to re-awaken and renew their bond that was not only in a bed, but in the one life they shared. Time away, visiting his parents, he hoped would bring his anger-weary family together again. For now, it was his wife he needed to tame. To him, she was a wildcat, demanding his respect and needing his love. Taking her in his arms, his love willingly led the way.

• • •

During their entire stay at his parent's house, his mother and father filled their days with activity. It left Candelaria longing for some time to herself. One day, the opportunity presented itself. Her mother-in-law was taking the children to a birthday party, so Candelaria declined the invitation to join them. Her father-in-law took Big Jimmy horseback riding around their expansive property. Thankful for the quiet time alone, Candelaria decided to go for a walk. Past the corral, she heard water trickling nearby, hidden within willows and berry thickets. A trail followed the course of the unseen stream, so she walked alongside it, discovering it led to a pond. It was only a man-made reservoir, but cattails grew tall along its edges and frogs croaked from their hiding places amidst the algal-green mud and muck. The sun was a bright glare on the water's surface. The pond gave off a slight, sour odor, but Candelaria sat beside its edge.

Earlier in their stay, she overheard her husband mention to his dad about her temper. She was ashamed, but could hardly blame him for unloading his troubles onto his father. Her in-laws had their own tense moments. Alice shared with her the grievances she had with her husband, Tim, saying that he would have so much work to do, right when she needed him most. At dinner one evening, Candelaria teased her father-in-law about it and, though she regretted it at first, it elicited a round of light-hearted comments. Soon, they were all laughing at what was really only human nature.

Candelaria reflected on this for a while. She observed that all couples had something, all families. No couple, no family was perfect, she learned. They each had something that either challenged them or brought them great suffering. God was not picking on her family or any one family. At the big gatherings, and the Smith clan had the biggest she had ever seen, she knew that all those who were there, had some kind of problem, whether themselves, as a couple, or their children.

She told herself, "If I were a writer, I would write about this and help others to see it, too."

The sun warmed her and, though the air was cool, she became sleepy and thought of going back to the house. A momentary hesitation, however, held her long enough in place to witness something curious. In her drowsiness, she heard and felt someone walk up to her, yet saw no one. A ripple ran across the surface of the pond, though no wind had blown. A mouse, fidgety and quick, came out of hiding and stuffed cattail fluff into its cheeks, then scurried off. It came out again and collected more fluff, hopping away in a hurry. It did this several times. Candelaria felt as though someone sat beside her, showing her something. She struggled to grasp what was being shown, but the feeling faded away. She knew she was "alone."

Back at the house, Candelaria lay down and took a nap. She pondered over the experience as she lay quietly and soon fell asleep. A dream began, in which she was awake, walking out of the house, like it really appeared that day. She walked over to the pathway that led from the horse barn toward the small pond. All around, were gathered a dozen or more winged beings, like angels, though some were also animal-like. She sat by the water in her dream and one of these beings sat beside her. A parting of the sky appeared before them and an enormous lion came, walking across the water toward where she sat. The mouse came out, though it was not a mouse in the dream. It was she, Candelaria. She was gathering the downy cattail fluff. The being that sat next to her said something so clear, yet so odd, like a hushed murmuring whispered underwater. Candelaria believed it was very important.

CHAPTER SIX

The 42nd Annual Pine Way Settler's Day Picnic brought the Hart family and other wartime families to the picnic grounds. People carried bags and they hefted baskets. Maybe a blanket or a tarp was carried in their arms. Big Jimmy sat astride his bay gelding, Theodore. Little Jimmy sat in front, his cowboy hat, boots, and jeans matching those his daddy wore. A very pregnant Candelaria walked beside her aging horse, Castanets, with Rosalita seated alone in the saddle. Smiles from onlookers were met with "good morning" and "fine day for a picnic, isn't it?" Once they arrived, Rosalita sat taller in the saddle and Little Jimmy perked up, having spotted their playmates gathering at the far side of the clearing.

Each year, someone told a story at the picnic, either a memory or something pertaining to the town's history. People looked forward to it, regarding it as an important part of the annual festivities. Picnickers sat on blankets and tarps, with picnic supplies close at hand. Announcements were made and any surviving founders of the community received acknowledgement. One of them was absent this year, Harrison Stewart, who could not attend the picnic due to illness, his daughter-in-law, Adelaide Stewart, explained. She reassured everyone that her mother-in-law was at home taking care of him.

Addie's son, Howard, had accompanied his fiancée, Mary Weatherby. He announced earlier that he planned to tell the story of his grandfather and the early beginnings of Pine Way. Grinning and shy beside his lady friend, he stood, then left her side. His mustache felt extra prickly and his undershorts extra itchy. Once he climbed the crate steps that led up to the flatbed trailer, which served as their stage, his discomfort went away and he began to tell his tale.

• • •

Howard's grandfather, Harrison Stewart, was an enterprising young man when he and his new bride, Phoebe Adano, drove their wagon into town. They were followed by a freight wagon containing the printing press for the town's newspaper. The person who had contacted Harry, said the little frontier town was called Pine Way, but the sign read differently. The Way? He pondered the name, but it soon mattered little to him. Townspeople came out of the few shops. Others approached the wagon, shaking his hand, so happy to see him and his wife. They were all talking and shouting and smiling at once.

Aided off the wagon, Harry and Phoebe were promptly given a tour of the town while their trunks and parcels were taken to their room in the way station. The bright sunlight was gleaming from metal surfaces and puddles, everything washed clean from recent rainfall. Things were looking very promising to Harry Stewart. He imagined their new home, their growing family, and the many opportunities which awaited him and his wife.

The shopkeeper, Thomas McGrew, asked, "How're we gonna get this contraption off the wagon and into the building?"

He and his son, Ulysses, circumnavigated the freight wagon.

"It's kinda big," Thomas remarked.

Not wanting to deflate the celebratory nature of their arrival, Harry excused himself. The teams needed to be taken out of their harnesses and he needed to see to his wife. Other people began gathering around the freight wagon, marveling at the printing press, not as large as they had imagined, but appearing impossibly enormous to unload. Standing off to the side, Harry doubted he would ever forget how far they had to haul "the blasted thing," a phrase he used often during their long trek from the coast, up the delta, up the valley, and ascending into the mountains.

The wagons were unloaded, the teams led over to the livery stable by the young men who worked there and the teamster who was hired to manage the horses, so Harry relaxed. Once the printing press was set in place and the sliding shop door of the building slid back into position, he felt the greatest of his burdens lifted from his worried brow. Lifting another burden, he remembered someone telling him before he left the coast that additional supplies were due to arrive by the end of the week, items specifically for printing a newspaper. While he preferred to call it *The Pine Way Weekly Journal*, he figured if they wanted it to be named *The Way Weekly*, he would happily accommodate them.

Taking his pocket watch from its little pocket on his vest, he checked the time, for no other reason than to admire his wedding gift from his wife and its tender inscription, "To my dearest Harrison, Phoebe." He closed his eyes and sighed, for another burden awoke to remind him of something else he had forgotten.

At this point in Howard's version of his grandfather's story, he pointed to his father, Tucker Howard Stewart, seated with his wife and family on a red and green plaid blanket nearby. Howard asked him, very respectfully, to show the audience his watch. His brother, Dewey, was nervously looking on, because the boys in the family were preparing to sign up to go to war and planned to spring the news on their parents while at the picnic.

Tucker Howard stood up, smiling and waving. He tugged on the watch fob to draw the watch out of its pocket on his vest. He held it up to show everyone that he had become the proud owner of that wedding gift from his mother to his father. The other picnickers applauded, some whistled, others hurled comments intended to bring laughter, though went unappreciated.

A fight broke out amongst the children playing by the edge of the forest. All ages and sizes, girls and boys, were gathered around to watch and egg-on the two most vociferous opponents, Little Jimmy and not-so-little Tucker James. Vying for Sylvia Cadwallader's attentions was already in the making at ages seven and eight.

Howard's story was temporarily postponed while parents ran to yank their children back to their picnic spots. Among them were his sisters, Marjorie and Lois, red-faced and embarrassed for being discovered and admonished publicly for yelling the loudest and most egregious comments.

Dottie McGrew and Rosalita Hart were very proud of Buster Smith, who, despite his chipped-tooth speech difficulties, cut quite a figure in their young, adoring eyes.

Children were laughing at Buster when he said, "Ssthtop! Ssthop it, you kidssth! Thomebody help me with thesth boyssth!"

He ended the fight when he grabbed Little Jimmy by the scruff of the neck and dragged him toward his father. Big Jimmy took over from there with his own string of oaths, directed toward his son for the benefit of anyone who dared to say he was a lax parent. He was not about to let his son get away with anything, at least not while people were watching. Privately, he was tickled by his son's feistiness.

In the meantime, Howard took the opportunity, cuing his younger brother, Dewey, to inform their mother of their plans to join the service together, right after Howard's wedding.

Their shocked mother unabashedly yelled to her husband, "Tucker Howard! Get back here!" Which he did, with his youngest son in tow, only to learn of his other two son's plans to go to war.

At the same time, poor Mary Weatherby burst into tears, face reddening rapidly, handkerchief at the ready, her white-gloved hands balled into fists as she glared at Howard. She told him she felt "like a betrayed woman, practically abandoned at the altar," before she had arrived, and would not speak to him ever again, all the while giving him an earful. Apparently, she had not gotten "all dressed up for nothing" if not to show the world her intentions. She would not have had her hair done, if it were not to be accompanied to the picnic grounds, arm in arm, by her fiancé, Howard My-Name-Is-Mud Stewart, which was how he felt by that point. Regardless, the crowd wanted to hear the story.

Howard tried to smooth things with Mary and his parents, when his own brothers turned on him, being the eldest son, blaming him for such a ridiculous idea as joining up at all. "And think of our poor, dear mother!" they said. Howard refused to take the stage until he had everyone's full attention, itchy shorts, prickly mustache, stiff collar, and all.

His parents, however, were still trying to contend with their youngest.

"I don't wanna apologize to him!" said Tucker James. Dirty and disheveled, face begrimed with tears and sweat, he claimed, "Sylvia's my friend!"

Little Jimmy said, "I saw her first!"

Lois had observed that Sylvia, all of six years of age, had been flirting with the both of them, plying her feminine wiles, as per her mother's own misguided behavior, causing the whole thing. Although, Little Jimmy did say something mean to another boy present, five-year-old Forty Sumner.

"Why do you always have your hand on your wanger?!" he asked Forty.

Tucker James had allegedly stepped in to defend his friend, who ran home crying, his own parents not having attended the picnic.

Ted and Henry Stewart, wishing to escape their parent's wrath, ran after Forty Sumner, under the pretense they were making sure he got home all right. The following order was shouted after them by their aggrieved mother to "get right back here, you two, you hear me?!" She had not the gift of telling the future, for if she had, those words would have meant much more to her, being as they would sign up together in 1944. Howard and Dewey would return home safely, whereas Ted and Henry would return from the war in coffins. Thankfully, this was not yet known and Howard, having calmed his family, resumed his place on the stage and his enjoyable story, which took everyone's mind off the issue at hand, namely, the war.

• • •

Harrison Stewart was painfully aware he had forgotten to purchase his wife a wedding gift. Slipping his watch back into its secure pouch on his vest, he dared to venture the idea that, perhaps, he was enough. Swiftly dismissing that guilt-inducing thought, he remembered being told it was supposedly some sort of custom in her family. In short, he did not have a gift for her. He made up an excuse that sufficed as they said their goodbyes to the crowd of weeping women and bragging and guffawing men back home, that her gift was already waiting for her when they would arrive in Pine—The Way.

Henry Henry asked him, "Certainly you and your wife would like to go to your room and get comfortable, rest up for supper?"

Distracted, due to being at a complete loss for wedding gifts, Harry fretted aloud.

"No worry!" The way station owner assured him, "Trust me. You and your wife are in good hands."

Harry was led over to the way station while his wife was distracted by women surrounding her with their own round of welcomes. He arranged to have her gift placed in their room, a hand-carved picture frame made by Henry Henry, who loved woodcarving, and a lovely knit shawl, crocheted by Henrietta.

Through the years, Harry Stewart never forgot that day. He was endlessly impressed with the talents of these courageous frontier people he had joined in the joyful tending of their town. The townsfolk were pleased and thankful for the paper, which went from being *The Way Weekly* to *The Pine Way Weekly Journal*, after all.

"My grandfather," Howard said, "was fortunate to have a young journalist return home, fresh from the strife and struggle in Mexico, a college graduate, at that, named Herman Mendoza. Herman was an invaluable addition to their newspaper staff of one, namely, my grandfather."

At the mention of Herman's name, the gray-haired man waved from his small blanket where he sat off to the side with his brother, Jesse, and his sister-in-law, Ev. Howard led his audience in a small round of applause. Since many of the children were making a point to say it was past lunch time, Howard concluded with the lesson to his grandfather's story.

"My grandfather, Harrison Stewart, has never regretted being so foolish as to believe in himself and come to this beautiful valley and start a new life."

CHAPTER SEVEN

Howard was relieved no one at the picnic pressed him for the tragic portion of his grandfather's story. According to his grandfather, it not only involved the death of four people, but the death of their town. The retelling of the darkest period in Pine Way and Edenville's history, revealed the darker side of his grandfather. He likened the incident to chopping off the top of a garden plant when it was beginning to flower and produce fruit. With the cessation of growth, came the diminution of its powers. Thereafter, his grandfather warned, Pine Way's future led only to stagnation, foretelling a slow shriveling into decay.

The dreaded incident to which he referred had taken place in 1899. It was early in the morning and the townspeople were beginning their day. Ulysses McGrew had opened his father's store. Activity in the post office and telegraph station had begun with Cedric Cadwallader opening the window shades. Harry and Herman were getting the next weekly edition out, when, not one, but two shots rang out, supposedly the first ever heard in their peaceful valley. Harry hurried outside and saw people running past and heard women crying and screaming. He ran back to get his jacket and out the door he flew.

Not long after that unfortunate day, Henrietta gave up on life. Since her children, Walter Henry and Lulabelle, were unable to take over, her dying words to her nephew were, "It's all yours and Walter's, when he's of age."

At little over eighteen years of age, Timothy Hart and his new bride, Alice, became the new owners of the blacksmith shop, the livery stable, and the way station. Alice was not much of a cook, being very young and inexperienced, so Phoebe Stewart stepped in to lend a hand. A regrettable decision, for Harry, having heard the whispered complaints over the new menu. People were displeased when their usual fare was replaced with "slop they'd as soon throw to the dogs." All was not lost, for Alice soon became proficient at the large cookstove, thanks to her mother's help. Poor Phoebe Stewart was relegated to the housekeeping tasks, since Estefana Garcia and her daughter, Ev Mendoza, quit the way station and moved into their own home.

Howard had heard many stories from his Grandma Stewart regarding life in a way station. Seated on a picnic blanket, reflecting on those stories, he thought somebody ought to write them down. But, as he stared into space, recalling the last of those stories, when the way station partially burned and was later abandoned, it struck him how precious it was, a building in which so many lives had come together. It was gone for good, he believed. His grandmother and grandfather were probably not long for the world, he thought. But, he hoped their stories would endure. Like the way station, they could suffer a similar fate, he feared, and become abandoned and forgotten, too.

A welcomed round of activity ensued when the picnic moved on to the games and prizes portion. Mary Weatherby sat patiently beside her intended, Howard Stewart, for which he was thankful. A small group gathered around them, asking to hear more of the story. He braced himself, wondering what exactly "more" meant. They asked him to share what he knew about how the town became Pine Way. Fortunately, for Howard, the Hart family packed up and moved their belongings to where the relay races were being held, since Little Jimmy and Rosalita wanted to participate. Discovering it was their presence that gave rise to his nervous itching attacks, Howard soon relaxed. To the best of his memory, he finished his Grandpa Stewart's long-winded tale.

The dark turn of events, which Howard skirted around in his rendition, brought many changes. Along with these changes, rose the clamor regarding the town's name. It was found necessary to call a town meeting. They met in the Catholic church. Howard's grandfather presided, calling the meeting to order with his new gavel. He admired its craftsmanship, his name delicately carved into the wood. He was proud to put it to work.

At this point in the story, Howard, who was lying on his side, an elbow propping him up as he gnawed away at a drumstick, sat up and dug into a bag he had brought. He drew out his grandfather's treasured gavel, delighting his listeners. Ooh's and ahh's were heard, along with a few belches by the men, and the women, who had enjoyed too much chicken, potato salad, and chocolate cake.

Howard described the meeting that took place long ago in the tiny Catholic church that no longer existed. Within the dimly lit building, his grandfather's booming voice addressed the townsfolk.

"Now, we are all very grateful," he said, "to the first settlers of this area for building its very first establishments, which welcomed many a weary traveler to and from these beautiful mountains."

Like his grandfather had always done in the telling of his story, Howard did likewise. He extended his arm to sweep through the air, pointing out the mountains to his enthralled listeners. Having their attention, he continued the story, adding flourishes he knew his grandfather would have enjoyed.

"I, for one," Harrison continued, "can tell everyone truthfully how thankful I am for the beautiful brick buildings that have become our town. I especially thank you for inviting my wife, Phoebe, and I to come live here amongst the nicest folks we've ever known, and start a newspaper." He stopped to clear his throat, rap the gavel again, then added, "Phoebe never imagined she'd be called upon to help run a way station. We're both very thankful you gave her a chance. But, what we're needing to face is the fact that, well, I don't know of a single one of us whose gratitude has ever extended to the naming of this town by Henry Henry. So—"

Harrison Stewart's treasured gavel was pounded several more times to restore order. Forty-five people had attended, all talking at once, plus children outside allowed to run amok. He rued the decision to offer refreshments to get people to attend, for now they had a crowd. He held the gavel, determined to lead the town council, and proceeded, carefully choosing his words.

"I have not lived here as long as some of you," he said. "I don't even consider myself a pioneer, but I know I have missed Henry and Henrietta Henry just as much as the rest of you."

It was then that he gave up and said, "Oh, hell, everybody's been calling this place Pine Way for years now, why not make it official? Everyone in favor, say 'aye' and raise your right hand."

Addressing Ulysses McGrew, he said, "No, Uly, your right hand! The other one!"

People laughed at poor Ulysses McGrew, who sat up straight, blinking his eyes in embarrassment.

Nearly all agreed, and those who did not, could at least admit it was easier to take the old sign down than to think up a new name.

Phoebe Stewart waved her hand in the air to get her husband's attention. He asked her to stand and, with an air of authority, she commented, "Henrietta Henry pulled that sign out after the death of her husband. Even she liked the name of Pine Way," which was true.

Henrietta wagged her head, along with a pointed and determined index finger at her husband for naming their beloved home in such a way, saying, "It's blasphemous!"

Phoebe further settled the matter in a way that endeared her husband's pride in her. She said, "After all, Pine Way is its natural name. We didn't choose it. It chose us."

Applause followed and the meeting was summarily adjourned. The townsfolk of the officially proclaimed "Pine Way" descended upon the punch bowl. They scooped up slices of cake and then their children, once out in the night air.

Howard's listeners were a bit disappointed, asking him, "That was it?"

Howard nodded his head and said, "Yes, that's how the town got its name."

His listeners, fortunately for him, were much too weary and stuffed to pester him for more. They sauntered over to the relay races to join the cheering crowd. Several children hopped toward the finish line in the gunny sack race. Onlookers cheered and

Howard turned his gaze away to find himself alone with his fiancée, Mary.

She had grown impatient awaiting the end of his story. Resigning herself to their fate, she spoke her heart about his news to enlist.

"Oh, Howard," she said, "I can't bear for you to leave."

Later in the day, the fun and games over, blankets and parcels were collected. The tired crowd dispersed and filed out of the picnic grounds, some walking, some on horseback, others in their cars. Candelaria's father, Jesse Mendoza, being the school janitor, was asked to clean up after the picnickers. His brother, Herman, and his Uncle Dexter Shows-His-Guns volunteered to help. Walter Henry stayed behind and Little Jimmy begged to stay and help out as well. His parents agreed.

Many dubbed this picnic the best they ever had. Though it would be the last, they looked forward to the following year's all the same.

A small group of people stopped along the way to visit the Edenville Community Cemetery and pay their respects to the settlers no longer living. This informal tradition was viewed as a respectful conclusion to each year's Settler's Day Picnic. Some brought flowers, albeit artificial or wilting ones to adorn the graves of their forebears.

The usual practice was to begin by mentioning the history of the entrance gate to the cemetery. It was an iron gate fashioned by Timothy Hart, his blacksmithing skills augmented by creativity and vision. The four lone graves Timothy and Alice saw back then were graced with the delicate ironwork of Timothy's thoughtfully rendered gift. It stood in honor of his parents and his aunt and uncle who were buried near one another, each couple on either side of the entry path.

"It's like walking into a church," Alice commented tearfully when her husband installed the gate. She lightly outlined the wrought iron vines and blooms that wound around the beautiful iron gateway he had made. She looked into his eyes and thanked him as she smiled and said, "One day, you and I will be buried here, side by side. I'll be proud to set in a field with such a lovely gate as this to welcome everyone."

Timothy took her hand in his and placed his other on the gateway, both looking on at their sad futures, innocent of what lie in store for them beyond death.

The present-day visitors, arriving at the cemetery after the picnic, proceeded from the entrance, visiting the graves in each row. Headstones were read aloud and unusual or especially memorable ones drew a tear as flowers were placed beside them. No longer were there only four lone graves, for many had since died, being the only cemetery in all of Pine Way and Edenville.

The peaceful sojourners discovered that the old town's rustic burial ground was not only like a church, but, as one child remarked, "It's like a neighborhood."

The group of visitors drew together to discuss this poignant observation, directing one another's attention to the names so familiar to them: Henry, Hart, Smith, Cadwallader, Jones, Walker, McGrew, Garcia, Mendoza, and even the name, Shoseegan, which only a few had known. They were glad to have attended the picnic that day and to have followed it up with a visit to the town's cemetery. Reassured to see it was "like a neighborhood," they found comfort knowing that, even in death, the townspeople they once knew, but had lost, were still neighbors in old Pine Way.

CHAPTER EIGHT

Walter Henry missed Timothy Hart. Tim was someone from the old Pine Way days few were left who remembered, as evidenced by their scarcity at the picnic. He was disappointed. He had also wanted to join the Hart family on their trip, but was not invited. He brooded over it in the barn one morning.

Big Jimmy asked, "You ain't still pouting over that, are you Walt?" He stood facing the older man with a pitchfork in hand, adding, "I told you I was sorry. I had no idea you wanted to go."

"You didn't even ask," said Walter Henry.

Annoyed, Big Jimmy said, "Oh, you wouldn't have liked being in the car with my wife and kids with all their squabbling. You know that."

Changing the subject, Walter Henry asked, "So, how is ole Tim, anyway?"

"He's doin' fine," said Big Jimmy. "Coughs a lot—He smokes too damn much! Gonna burn up his whole spread if he don't quit!" He pitched some hay into one of the stalls and got a far-off look in his eyes. "They got a beautiful place," he said. "It sits up there just below the hills with all that tall grass. It's real pretty. I don't know how he did it, but it's a beautiful place."

Walter Henry was tempted to say, "I wish I could've seen it," but let his disappointment fade. He was not one to hold a grudge or throw a fit, so he went back to work. Reminded of the family and their frequent bickering, he figured it was time to count his blessings. Since their return, there was one change that took place which he appreciated, though would never say so.

He was an unmarried man and had no children, so the rest of the family's waning presence in the barn gave him a welcomed respite from the usual fussing and arguing. He had no idea why, himself, but Big Jimmy's wife spent little to no time at the blacksmith shop and livery stable since they came home and, with her, went the children. The days went a bit easier on the old man's nerves. He thought Candelaria was an edgy woman from whom he never knew what to expect. He preferred a peaceful atmosphere in the barn, especially around the horses.

Candelaria was gradually leaving the business to her husband without saying why, though Big Jimmy had his suspicions. She became more interested in the Mexican farmworkers who lived nearby in their own community recently built. Its residents light-heartedly dubbed the collection of hastily constructed shacks, "Villa Borracho," meaning Drunkard Town. One was a school friend of his wife's, Esther Chavez, whose daughter, Socorro, was one of Rosalita's best friends.

Big Jimmy was pleased to see his daughter with her friends, not only Socorro, whom they called, "Coco," but also the McGrew's daughter, Dottie, and the youngest Stewart girls, Marjorie and Lois. They would pet the horses and ooh and aah over them, though never want to ride them. Either their hair was done, their nails, or they had on new clothes.

He felt awkward with his daughter's emerging daintiness. She spent more time with her mother and the other girls, all of them talking at the same time, and "all in one cloud of perfume," he commented. Rosalita was becoming a young lady, which called into action all sorts of special fuss and attention he barely fathomed and occasionally found intolerable. He failed to understand. He never had a sister and his female cousins on the Smith side grew up far away. When his daughter and her friends got together for a sewing party, he was outnumbered and, evidently, out of style, for one minor gesture on their part told him so.

He asked one simple question, "What do you need all this stuff for?"

His daughter rolled her eyes and said, "Oh, Daddy!"

"I never seen so many frills and gewgaws." he said.

Not only his daughter, but his wife ganged up on him. Rosalita stuck her tongue out at him before she closed the door to her room, which she no longer shared with her brother. His wife followed suit with an, "oh, Daddy," of her own and a roll of the eyes as she playfully sashayed toward her daughter's room.

"Hey! Come 'ere!" He gave his wife a sharp spank and added, "You behave yourself. I'm gonna have to have a private talk with you." He was grinning big. Well, he supposed he could adjust, but there were limits.

His precious Rosalita insisted she be called, "Rosa." Having become a teenager, she was learning to cook and sew and, while his fatherly back was turned, she became a young woman. What disturbed him most was that she was drawing interest from boys in Pine Way and Edenville. The braids were gone, the cuffed jeans, and the wartime hand-me-downs and make-do's for both his children. Her hair, dark-brown like her mother's, was cut short and curled into something they called a "permanent," which some man named Tony had invented, he assumed.

School dances were announced for every occasion, school events for every season, and Candelaria loved it. Although, she did tell her husband she saw a look on Rosa's face, too, maybe a roll of the eyes, when Rosa said, "Oh, Mother!" Candelaria felt a tad old, herself, as she and her husband commiserated over the fact one evening.

"Sometimes, I feel like I'm in the way, like an embarrassment," Candelaria said.

"Well, I don't feel much better," Big Jimmy complained. "I'm just an old fool to them now, I guess."

Their son was no longer "Little Jimmy." He grew fast after he turned eleven and sprouted whiskers. His voice changed, too. Calling him "little" no longer felt right, so he became, "Jim." Big Jimmy, who was not that big, having taken after his mother's side of the family, became simply, "Jimmy." The toys were gone and life seemed different, quiet, almost too quiet, Jimmy warned his wife.

He missed having small children. He often wondered what life would have been like had their last two sons survived. The first one was named and baptized, then went to sleep one night and never woke up again. Jimmy had never seen such a tiny coffin. Walter Henry made it himself, adding some carvings of flowers on the lid. His wife said she wanted him buried in the Indian cemetery, saying they would look after their baby boy. Who "they" were, Jimmy had no idea. The child was a mystery, like he was only passing through their lives. When a second baby died, a couple or three years later, it seemed to Jimmy that the child was only visiting, as if only staying for a time before returning home again.

He visited the graves once, only to find his wife already there, laying her arms across both little mounds as if she were holding her babies in her arms beneath the comforting pines. Long after the flowers and other adornments in the burial ground disappeared, the tiny headstones remained, so "Baby Hart" and "Joseph Hart," could always be found. Months passed and Jimmy could barely remember them. He was afraid to stop visiting the graves, for fear he might forget them altogether.

He could hardly stand it anymore and worked with the big outfits down in the valley as often as he could. They needed the money and, like his partner, Walter Henry, he needed the breathing room.

Jim began helping out with the business, which prompted Jimmy to announce one day that it was time for his son to learn the trade. Not only did Jimmy hope it would keep his son's hands better occupied, instead of using them to make fists with which to hit people, he realized the value in teaching his son everything he knew.

"If you learn a trade, Son, you'll always have a job," was Jimmy's wisdom on the subject.

He observed that Jim was growing tall after he started high school and was drawing attention from the opposite sex, young women whose own eyes had a look all their own. Whereas, Jimmy was once the favorite of the ladies, his son moved up in the world. The eyes that no longer gazed Jimmy's way, fondly admired his son, followed by, "Oh...he's so handsome..." Their eyes also rolled, telling Jimmy something altogether different.

He knew when his son was sneaking out of his bedroom, popping the screen out and stealing away into the night, but it mostly resulted in talk, so Jimmy let it go. He and his wife recalled the times they got caught sneaking out of the house to be with friends when they were teenagers, which brought a few laughs. However, Jimmy found it worrisome, telling his wife, "I was a young man once, myself. I think I know what that boy's up to." Irregardless of her tensed-up, teeth-gritting look, he said, "He's got to know he can't just go sneaking around behind our backs!"

It happened when one girl in particular, came over to their house, the Cadwallader girl. He tried to remember her name, Syl, or something like that. He caught them together in Jim's room. The incident disturbed him. They were all involved and worked up, kissing each other on Jim's bed. Jimmy could have stood by and watched had he not reacted so quickly. Without hesitating, he sent the girl home.

"You git your caboose on outta here, little lady!" he said.

The words came out so fast, he was unable to stop them, the same words his own father said one time when Jimmy was alone with a girl. He asked himself how it happened. When did he become his father? Somehow, somewhere along the line, he not only became like his father, he had become Public Enemy No. 1: a parent. He became old after his fortieth birthday. Jimmy never felt like a parent when their children were, well, children. Back then, they were a family. He was shocked. He and his wife had become parents and the kids they raised had turned into strangers.

CHAPTER NINE

One time, while walking home from the blacksmith shop and livery stable, Jimmy caught a boy trying to climb through the window of Rosa's bedroom. He saw legs and boots on the outside and, upon hurrying to his daughter's room, caught her helping him. Enemy or not, Jimmy told Candelaria it was time to set some rules.

"If they're old enough to be carryin' on, I figure they're old enough to become grown up in every other way!"

Since the war ended, parents were confronted with things their own parents never experienced. It was a different era. Children were different, expecting things from life their parents had no idea how to provide. Situations were different. Whereas Josiah Hart's day had ended with the closing of the frontier, Jimmy Hart's day was ending with the modernization of rural life, losing its slow pace and neighborly connections. They used to help each other and meet up at the general store or the post office. He used to know all his neighbors and they used to know him. It was no longer that way. People kept to themselves, listening to their radios and eating frozen food, he suspected.

Children were no longer satisfied to do chores, maybe feed the chickens or help cut firewood. With the changing times came the need for fashionable clothes and hair products, music and entertainment.

The battle between worlds ensued. Parents rose to the challenge, so it was arranged to hold a meeting at the school to discuss these very issues. Jimmy and Candelaria debated whether it was worth it to go and leave their hormonally active teenagers alone at home. In the end, they decided to go, hoping to get some advice as the white flag was raised in the Land of Parenthood.

Arriving at the meeting, Jimmy and Candelaria entered the cafeteria where the program was being held. A guest speaker, Doctor Something-Or-Other, was coming, they heard one man say. They stood by the door, looking for people they knew from their own school days. Jimmy recalled dating a couple of them. Candelaria whispered to him that she wished they had stayed home, when, to his relief, he found someone he wanted to talk to, his own brother.

Jefferson brought his new wife, shotgun wedding, Jimmy recalled. It happened fast, right after the war. They had a couple of kids already, he noted.

"Howdy, brother!" said Jimmy. "What brings you to a parent's meeting about teenagers?"

They shook hands and offered up a slap on the back to each other, joking about how times had changed, reminiscing about the good ole days and commenting on the latest news of their father's passing.

"Well, you know my wife and I both work at Spring Hill," Jefferson said. "We thought it'd be a good idea to attend."

When did Jefferson become responsible? Jimmy wondered, only having known him as—

"Boy, I didn't think our old man would last as long as he did," said Jefferson. "He smoked like a freight train, puffin' and puffin'. Remember? Gee whiz! Oh well. I'm sure glad he came out here before then," and he talked on and on. Occasionally, a shot of spittle struck Jimmy, due to his brother talking so fast through his crooked front teeth.

When did he get to be so gabby? Jimmy wondered about that, too. It wore him out trying to listen to it all. He was glad the program was finally going to get started. Mentioning their father's death made him feel uncomfortable. Too many loved ones had died in too short a time, he recalled, which made him squirm.

Jefferson was referring to their parent's only visit back to Pine Way one Christmas after Jimmy and Candelaria went to visit them. Jefferson had gotten back from the war, though remained living elsewhere. His girlfriend got pregnant. Her brothers came for Jefferson's "life and limb on a barbecue grill," he had confided in Jimmy. He said they planned to skin him alive and cook him on the spot and eat him, too, unless he married their sister. They had a preacher handy, waiting in their car. The newlyweds came to Edenville to live. They got good jobs at the Spring Hill Residence & Infirmary, he as the head cook, since he was a cook in the service, and she as a nurse in the infirmary. She was a nurse in the service, stationed at the same military base where Jefferson was stationed.

When his parents learned of the marriage and a baby on the way, they came back to Pine Way for Christmas. Like a reunion, they had the whole family together, minus Jackson. Weeks before their arrival, Jimmy never saw his wife clean so much. Her mother and father helped out with new curtains on the windows and new upholstery on the living room furniture. They spruced up what was left of the garden.

Jimmy got teary-eyed and caught himself not paying attention to the meeting's guest speaker. He perked up, only to return to his wandering thoughts.

He realized their Christmas that year was one of those times he knew would never come again. Even his in-laws joined in the holiday festivities. Candelaria's brothers were not planning to visit that year. Walter Henry was invited, but he declined. Oh, well, Jimmy thought. He later heard that his father took a plate of food and visited with the quiet blacksmith over at the barn, which seemed to make them both happy, so everything turned out okay.

Before dinner, he had stepped out, or rather, was chased out of the kitchen by all the women. Jefferson left in his car, saying he had to hurry home to pick up the pies they forgot to bring with them. Jesse was dozing next to his jug of wine at one end of the sofa in the living room. Seeing Jim and Grandpa Tim privately conversing outside on the porch, Jimmy decided to sit on the other end of the sofa, maybe take a nap as well. The conversation in the kitchen faded into the background as the quiet discussion on the front porch became more distinct. He heard, "that goes in the oven after we take the turkey out," which were his wife's orders in the kitchen, before he heard, from out on the porch, "how do you know you're in love, Grandpa?"

Jimmy was grinning, but he knew the pain involved in such a question. No surprise to him it was about the Cadwallader girl. He shook his head and whispered, "Doggone it, boy, that ain't love." He could hardly blame his son. She was a pretty little thing, at that, he always thought. Something about her, though, gave him the willies. Two years younger than his boy, made her only...twelve? Well, maybe thirteen. He made a mental note to ask his wife about it. He was aware she disliked the girl and had some Spanish word she called her. Not a nice one, he was certain. But, he knew it expressed the same feeling he had about her. He knew Sylvia's parents in school and, though they were not bad people, he heard the rumors circulating and had seen the girl's red-eyed, staggering father. She was caught in the middle, having lost her mother, too, not that long ago, he recalled.

He shook his head, not wanting to think about those kinds of things anymore, worried enough about his son being home alone. Rosa was supposed to be at a friend's.

"Oh, Lord," he muttered.

Candelaria glanced his way, concerned. "What?" she whispered.

He leaned toward her and said, "We need to get home."

They stood up together and left the cafeteria in the middle of the parent's program. The value in going, as it turned out, was more about visiting and catching up with town folks than it was about learning anything they needed to know.

Jefferson and his wife hurried after them.

Jefferson asked, "Need a ride home?"

They got a lift as far as their driveway. Jimmy dreaded what they might find once they got to the house. He regretted going to that "damn silly meeting," he muttered to himself as they got out of the car. After a round of goodbyes, Jefferson and his wife drove away.

"Doggone it," said Jimmy.

"What? Doggone it, what?" asked Candelaria.

"Never mind," Jimmy said. "Must be my corns actin' up."

He took his wife's hand and leaned toward her to kiss her as they strolled along in the dark. But, after a while, he asked, "Did you get a look at Bobby Cadwallader?" That family was on his mind.

"I did," answered Candelaria. "He was drunk when he got to the school. The principal asked him to leave."

"Hmph," said Jimmy. "No wonder I didn't see him in the cafeteria."

They were silent for a minute, before Jimmy asked, "How about that ole Patty McGrew? She was all decked out. I guess Clarence hit it big with that new business of his. Walt said they're talkin' about building themselves a big fancy house up on Spring Hill."

They both wagged their heads and tsked and whistled in dismay. However, they were shocked out of their anxious pleasantries, when they saw Sylvia Cadwallader walking up their driveway in the dark. She approached them, but went on past, never looking their way. An awful feeling came over Jimmy at the sight of her. Like a vision of Death from out of the shadowy depths, her ghostly form related to him his son's demise, and he felt himself grow pale and weak as the earth beneath his feet nearly fell away.

CHAPTER TEN

Candelaria and Jimmy stopped and looked at each other in surprise, about to say something, when they heard Rosa shouting, "Why'd you do it, Jim?! Why?! Oh, God!"

They ran the rest of the way, hearing Jim crying loudly. Their legs were in the way of their flight. Once they reached the porch, Rosa hurried out of the house to meet them. She was crying and shaking.

"It's about time you got here!" she said.

Jimmy entered the house and the nightmare began. In the bathroom at his left, his boy sat rocking back and forth, crying, and singing a native lullaby Jimmy's wife often sang when distressed. His son's left arm was bandaged. Blood was oozing between the gauze. Blood had also spattered the floor, the sink, and the walls. Jimmy rushed to hold his son while his mind was off in its own dream of death and sorrow, losing their two baby boys, then his father, then—

He shut the bathroom door and locked it, got more bandaging and a towel to hold down on his son's arm, but the bleeding continued unabated. He wanted to prevent his wife from seeing all the blood, but he knew he had to do more.

Candelaria had stayed outside on the porch, holding Rosa who was telling her what had happened. The information was lost on Candelaria. Her son's sobbing had reached her ears. She left Rosa's side to hurry into the house. Her eyes widened as she approached the bathroom. Rosa blocked her way to hold her back.

"Mom! No. No! Don't." Taking her mother's arm, she spoke to her in a low voice. "Let Dad take care of him," she said. "He'll know what to do."

Candelaria felt she would die from the pain in her heart, until the bathroom door opened and Jimmy said, "Get the car! We need to take him to the infirmary!"

Candelaria did as she was told. Jimmy carried their son out to the car. He had fainted. Candelaria got in back and helped to lay Jim on the back seat. She held his head in her lap, whispering comforting words she learned as a child that spoke her prayers and entreaties for his survival. Blood smeared the back of the seat, yet went unseen in the dark.

Rosa also sat in the back seat. She told her brother, "Hang on, Jim! We're taking you to the infirmary. You're gonna be okay."

Jimmy thrust another towel toward the back seat. "Keep it on his arm!" he said. "Press it down and hold it!"

He drove their old Buick so fast, he likely straightened every curve and flattened every bump in the road. His son had intentionally hurt himself. Jimmy wrestled to accept this shocking truth as he whispered, "Please, God, please!"

Rosa informed them, "I've seen this before, you know...Jim cutting himself."

Jimmy shut out what she said for fear he might get sick or break down from shock. He wanted to rewind the film and start over. But, he wondered how far back he would have to go. Wishing he had decided not to go to that meeting, he chided himself for not following his instincts. He knew they had better sense.

"What kind of father am I?" he said to himself. Tears welled in his eyes and he rubbed them with his sleeve, so he could see the road.

They reached the highway and crossed it, soon arriving at the infirmary. Once there, Jimmy leapt and, three stairs at a time, ran to the entrance in a panic. The night nurse read his face and listened to him relate what had happened. She ran down the hall to get a wheelchair, which Jimmy practically threw down the stairs to the car. When the nurse saw that Jimmy's son was unconscious, she hurried off once more.

"We're gonna need a stretcher," she said.

She returned, followed by two aides with a stretcher who took over carrying Jim inside, where he would finally be treated.

Jimmy and Candelaria, however, were kept out of it. Together with Rosa, they held one another close, saying whatever would reassure each other, especially Rosa.

When the doctor finally came out to the room that served as visiting room, waiting room, and social room, they turned their eyes up to him for an answer.

"Hello, Mr. Hart, Mrs. Hart," he said. He shook each of their hands. "Your son's going to be okay. We've stitched the cut. It went pretty deep. He's going to need to stay here, though, under observation, you understand."

"Yes?" Candelaria's agreement in a question spoke for her family.

The doctor explained, "He hasn't come to, just yet. He lost a lot of blood. It's been pretty traumatic, I'm sure for all of you, but he's still in danger."

He backed away as though to leave their side, but the Hart family stood up, still holding on to one another, ready to follow him.

Intervening, he said, "He won't be able to go home for at least a few days, until we know for sure he'll be okay and, hopefully, won't do this again."

The doctor tried to impress upon them the seriousness of the situation, explaining he had seen that type of behavior before, calling it, "self-harm." He referred to the multiple scars present on both of Jim's arms, but they were lost, their eyes wide with terror, evidently not understanding. So, in his report, he wrote, "self-inflicted cut," whereas he told Jim's parents that it was a "possible suicide attempt," because Jim almost died and needed time to recover.

"Go home and rest now," he said. "We'll take good care of your son."

He herded them toward the door, making sure they understood, "no visitors, under no circumstances should he be disturbed or upset in any way." He let them know that "our on-staff psychiatrist will be back in Monday morning, so he can talk to Jim and see what kind of treatment he needs."

"Psychiatrist?" Jimmy asked.

Not wanting to further upset them, the doctor instead concluded, "We'll call when your son's ready to go home. We can take care of the rest when you come back. All right?"

"Thank you" and "goodbye" never seemed so pitiful as they were then. Jimmy felt as though all his strength had gone away.

Lost and still in shock, he drove them home, slowly and in silence.

The streets in the small town were empty. Their whole world was in darkness, not only because there were no streetlights in town, but because the night had engulfed them. They were swallowed up with only two beams of light to guide them home.

At the house, they wearily dragged their feet indoors. Jimmy went to work cleaning the bathroom right away. Candelaria went into the kitchen with Rosa to pick up utensils scattered on the floor and wash dishes. Jimmy had never cleaned house a day in his life, but he cleaned that bathroom like he was trying to make up for all the things he never did.

Rosa came in to use the bathroom. Seeing her father scrubbing everything down, even where it did not need cleaning, she told him it was enough.

"Dad," she said.

"I'm almost done, sweetie." Jimmy scrubbed the wall behind the sink.

"Dad. Stop." Rosa went to grab the sponge out of his hand, but he broke down sobbing.

"Where did I go wrong?" he asked.

"Dad, it's okay. You did the best you could," she said.

Jimmy looked up at her with such a sadness. It were as though he had fallen into a pit and she was offering him a hand up, so he could climb out of it. He stood and set the bucket of sudsy water on the toilet with the sponge. He embraced his daughter, lending her his strength and love and showing her he would be strong and take care of things.

"Everything's gonna be all right," he said. "I'll make sure of it."

Rosa gave no details on what had taken place in their home before her parents arrived. She wanted to avoid hurting them more than they were already experiencing. Jim and Sylvia had argued and, in an angry huff, Sylvia left the house, which set off Jim, was all she told them.

Over time, as the incident her father referred to as, "the night Jim shook the rafters on the family home," became the first of a series of incidents, Rosa learned enough of what it meant to them as a family. It was an initiation of sorts into what she and her mother would come to know as, "Jim's secret."

Sylvia Cadwallader was no longer welcome in their house.

CHAPTER ELEVEN

Rosa was alone at the house when the telephone rang. "Yes, I'll be there at eight," she said. Scuffing across the wood floor in her slippers, hair in curlers and still wearing her muumuu, she hurried to her room to lay out her clothes for the day. Returning to the kitchen, she finished cleaning up after breakfast.

Rosa's friend, Dottie, encouraged her to become a beautician. Together, they planned to save their money for beauty college. Rosa's other friend, Socorro, had gotten pregnant and dropped out of high school. The young man married her, to the relief of her parents, Jorge and Esther Gutierrez. The Stewart girls, Marjorie and Lois, who were part of the old gang, left for college, vowing never to return to Edenville. Dottie was the only unmarried friend Rosa had remaining and, so, became her best friend.

Jim helped his dad with the business and he worked hard at his studies. He had become a man, was physically strong, taller than his father, and was participating in sports, most especially football, where he excelled. By his junior year, his popularity in school and with the girls had grown. From what his teachers and his coaches could tell, he was a normal teenager. However, something else was taking place. Jim was increasingly restless and irritable, sometimes angry and distant. The slightest thing would set him off. His presence at home deteriorated into an unbearable tension, which felt anything but normal to his parents.

What made matters worse, Candelaria thought, Jim had struck up a friendship with the sculptor who resided in the old general store next to the blacksmith shop. She knew the man, several years her junior. He was single, smoked marijuana, and rode a motorcycle. Sometimes he invited Jim along on rides up to Laketon, a mountain village where her father's mother yet lived.

She and Rosa were cleaning house on a rare day off from work. Rosa commented how Jim had taken the pictures down that were in his room. He had replaced them with those torn from magazines, pictures of motorcycles and horses, dogs—and one unusual image, which caught Candelaria's attention. It was of a Native American man with braided hair, holding a burning sage bundle, raised above him as though in offering. The background, a desert landscape with a colorful sunset mesmerized her. Rosa remarked on the motorcycle pictures.

"Just like his new hero, Tommy McGrew," she said.

Drawn out of her reverie over the Native American imagery, Candelaria asked her daughter, "Why would Jim be associating with that man? What are they doing up in the mountains?"

Dismissive, Rosa made light of it for reasons of her own. "Oh, Mom," she said, "some of the kids at school think he's cool."

No matter how hard she tried to keep the family together, the fraying relationship Candelaria had with her son collapsed into indifference on Jim's part. Her relationship with her husband became likewise difficult. Jimmy was gone for sometimes an entire week, working away from home. His return on weekends were unpleasant for reasons Candelaria avoided discussing. Starting a new job gave her a sense of independence, though only served to bring additional conflict to her strained marriage.

One day, she was on her way to work at the orchards. Wearing her husband's pants and shirt, her hair up in a bandanna, she stopped by the barn to get her work gloves. Jimmy's tight-lipped glance her way, told her he was mad.

She asked, "What?"

He said, "Nuthin'. Got nuthin' to say," and went about his own job saddling a horse.

Challenging him, Candelaria asked, "You got something against me going to work some place else?"

"No," he said. "What I don't like is you doin' farm work."

"What's wrong with farm work?" she asked.

"Farm work is for poor people, Larie. And, we're not poor."

"For your information, Jimmy, those 'poor people' are my people. Farm work is what my people do! So, if you will excuse me, I'm going to work," and she walked away.

Arguments between Candelaria and Jimmy were always present in their marriage, but they became more frequent. Failure to manage their son's issues on their own, consequently led to unremitting stress. The psychiatrist offered little help when they met with him, suggesting treatment too drastic to accept or too minimal to be of any use. Fortunately, there were few incidents of so-called suicide attempts, most of which they took care of at home or when Jim was at the barn. Calling them suicide attempts changed nothing, but it helped them to understand Jim's suffering. The alternative, to consider why he would intentionally cut himself was worse than incomprehensible, it was unthinkable.

Yet, Candelaria wanted to help their son. She asked Walter Henry if he would ask his sister, Lulabelle, to talk with Jim. Lulabelle had started a retreat center and practiced healing, which Candelaria believed could benefit their son.

This action on Candelaria's part brought resistance from her husband, who sternly argued, "I don't want her doin' any of her Indian magic on my boy! You should have asked me first instead of going behind my back!"

"What am I supposed to do, just watch our son cut himself to pieces?!" asked Candelaria.

"Now, why would you say a thing like that?!" Jimmy yelled back at her. "Of course, I don't want that, Larie!"

Candelaria continued to yell, saying, "First, you tell me I can't work where I want to, then you get mad like I can't even talk to the people I want to!"

Jimmy rubbed the palm of his hand across his jaw and shook his head. Walter Henry had already walked out of the barn, saying something about it being lunch time.

All Jimmy had to say was, "I'm sorry," but the words refused to come out of his mouth. They lost strength at the thought he had had enough, enough yelling and enough defending himself to a woman who refused to see what her anger was doing to them both.

What he failed to see was his wife's passion and determination, not directed against him, but toward something he was unable to see. Candelaria knew that not only her son and her marriage were breaking down, but their lives were slipping away.

She worried about their problems. Although, she gained some perspective learning of the strife under which other families struggled. The Stewart's, who had eight children, lost two sons in the war. She remembered the announcement at church during Mass. Father Jovial called on his parishioners to pray for the family during their time of great sorrow. The eldest daughter, June, whom Candelaria barely knew, had also died while giving birth. Even Mrs. Stewart had died. Candelaria especially empathized with the family when she heard of another son, Dewey, having made suicide attempts.

On different occasions, she encountered young men calling Dewey, "Dippity Dewey," or, "Dippy Dewey," which she found appalling. Conflicted over what to do in the moment, she was left with her guilt, because she said nothing to even the worst of these offenders. She slowly came to realize how alienated her own existence had become from the rest of the townspeople, except for other Mexicans, to whom she grew closer and appreciated for their love and support.

She still needed to address what was taking place in her own home, however, even if her efforts ended in failure. She attempted to check in on Jim, casually asking him about Sylvia. She wanted to be sure her son was all right as far as the girl was concerned. After all, they attended school together. She immediately regretted it, knowing she had made an awful mistake.

"Who cares about her!" he said to his mother in anger. "She's too young for me, anyway! Went and got all religious and everything!" He threw his hands in the air, like his father did, while striding across the living room. He opened and then slammed the front door on his way out.

After the shock of his outburst wore off, Candelaria covered her face with her hands and took a deep breath, saying, "Ay, Dios mio," and shook her head.

She asked Rosa, "Do you know if Sylvia's sleeping around?" Rosa told her, "Definitely not."

Candelaria knew Rosa had lied, and had proof, seen with her own eyes.

CHAPTER TWELVE

Late one afternoon, Candelaria left the house, following a path that led through the woods over to her mother's. It was 1951 and, her father, the children's Grandpa Jesse had passed away, leaving Candelaria to take care of her aging mother. She helped any way she could. Going for walks became an enjoyable pastime for them both, sometimes making it a picnic. Her mother, Ev, was nearly eighty, by that time, so their pace was slow and contemplative.

Candelaria appreciated spending time with her mother, which, in comparison to her home life, was quiet and serene. Her mother was the very picture of grace and simplicity, walking with her hands clasped behind her back, sometimes fashioning a walking stick from a tree branch. They would talk about the old days, sing songs, and laugh.

The shade was always welcome on warm, summer days, but, at that particular time of year, the air was much cooler. Leaves on the elms along the road, the maples in the woods, and the oaks were turning colors, yellow, orange, and red, piling in great drifts along the roadsides. The dampness from recent rains brought out the muddy, earthy odors of leaf mold and dead and decaying grasses and weeds. Puddles reflected the golden-yellow of leaves from above, along with the sky, so deeply azure.

Candelaria was about to share a minor tidbit of news, when she was startled by the sound of other voices. She and her mother looked at one another as the laughter of young people drew near.

She asked her mother, "Who could that be?"

Ev shrugged her shoulders and drew up her hands while shaking her head. "Don't know," she answered. She looked at her daughter, waiting, then questioned her in a whisper, "What do you want to do?"

The voices were familiar to Candelaria. She stood in place listening to them as they faded away. She and her mother both agreed the young people must have gone. Her mother was soon joking about it, being snoops over a couple of high school students walking home from school.

They continued walking along for at least another twenty or thirty minutes, stopping occasionally to look at something or comment on it.

Candelaria asked her mother, "Are you tired?"

"No," Ev answered. "Let's go to the livery stable. I haven't seen Jim in a long time." Her lower lip drew down in a childish pout.

Candelaria reluctantly agreed. "All right," she said with a noticeable sigh.

"What's the matter, mi hija?" Ev asked.

"I don't feel welcome there anymore," said Candelaria.

"What do you mean?" Ev was concerned.

Candelaria said, "Walter Henry gives me looks like he doesn't want me around." She stopped walking and grew sad.

Many was the time when Rosa laid her head in Ev's lap and poured out her grief over what took place in her family's home. So, as Candelaria stood there looking so sad, Ev knew why. Her daughter's family life was troubled, not only because of her grandson's problems, but because her daughter and her son-in-law were not getting along with one another. She hesitated saying anything, since her granddaughter told her in confidence.

They waited near the road, neither of them knowing what to do. A light breeze drifted through the woods. With it, came those same voices they had heard earlier. The young people, a boy and a girl, had evidently lingered somewhere nearby and were stomping through the leaves and talking.

Looking in that direction, Candelaria soon spotted them. "There they are!" she said, trying to keep her voice down.

Two people came up the embankment out of the woods and onto a back road nearby that led toward the houses in Edenville. They were less than a couple hundred yards away and showed not the slightest awareness that they were being watched. It was Sylvia Cadwallader and Tucker Stewart. Sylvia was buttoning the front of her blouse, putting on her sweater, and straightening her skirt, while he was tucking in his shirt and putting on his jacket. He pulled a leaf from her hair. They laughed and embraced one another.

Candelaria and Ev stood frozen to the spot, watching the two engage in some serious kissing like—

"Oh, Laria," said Ev while looking at her daughter. "I can hear your mind from here, mi hija. Don't think those thoughts."

Candelaria's eyebrows were down in her seriousness, so angry, appalled, as she asked her mother, "What kind of girl would do such a thing, Mamá?" She was flabbergasted.

Her mother kept shaking her head and cautioned her daughter. "We'd better go back to the house," she said. "This is no time to be seeing Jim."

Defiant, Candelaria said, "No, this is exactly the right time to see him." She wanted to tell her son what she had seen, so he would know what kind of girl Sylvia was and forget about her for good.

Ev was afraid, growing impatient, and told her daughter, "Come on." She began to walk back to her house, urging her daughter to listen. She tried to keep her voice down, but her daughter was ignoring her. "Forget about it!" she said. "It's none of our business!"

Still, Candelaria would not heed her mother's words, watching Tucker and Sylvia slowly walk away, his arm around her waist. They kissed again and Candelaria turned her head away, suddenly ashamed of herself for having watched them.

Ev gestured quickly with her hand for her daughter to come with her. "Laria!" she said in an emphatic whisper. "Ven aqui! Now! Let's go!"

It was then that the spell was broken and Candelaria finally surrendered. She believed that God showed her this for a reason, showed *her*, not her son. Recalling the time he was hurt by this girl, shocked her into realizing what a dangerous mistake it would be to tell him. It would be wrong, even cruel.

"You're right, Mamá," she said. "Let's go back to your house."

Regardless of their seriousness, Ev could not resist making fun of what they saw.

"Laria."

"What, Mamá?"

Making sure Candelaria was watching her, Ev repeated, "Laria. Laria, mírame. Look."

Candelaria looked her way as her mother began pretending she was kissing someone passionately, which got them both laughing again.

"Ahh, Life," Ev said with a smile.

Candelaria reminded her mother that Jim was planning to go to his Uncle Jefferson's house after school, so he was not at the barn. They talked about other things, what her mother wanted to do at the house, like clean out more of her husband's clothes and his personal possessions.

Ev remarked sadly, "I don't need those things."

They were quiet the rest of the way back to the house. Ev occasionally stopped to pick up a little stone or an interesting piece of wood and examine it. Candelaria renewed her obsession over what she had seen take place between Tucker and Sylvia. She had not talked to Tucker Stewart since he was a little boy. The idea of confronting him as a teenager about his behavior was out of the question. The reminder that he was a teammate of her son's and the brother of her daughter's friends, affirmed her decision to avoid saying anything to him, or anyone.

Stepping out of the drugstore one day, she nearly collided with Tucker and some of his teammates on their way to the diner. She noted he was grinning like he had some kind of private joke on his mind.

"I think it's going to rain," he said to his friends, and they laughed.

Tucker's rude comment closed the issue for Candelaria, who realized that, despite his actions, he was still a kid. She asked herself if she would continue to judge him and Sylvia or forgive them. She decided to forgive, for even she could remember what it was like to be young and in love.

CHAPTER THIRTEEN

Rosa was in the kitchen starting dinner for the family one evening. It was yet summer, too warm to cook, she thought, when Jim came home from working with their dad at the livery stable. He was in a hurry, slamming doors, uttering a string of oaths Rosa tried not to hear. She closed her eyes and, with hands upraised, melodramatically beseeched the heavens, silently praying for someone to marry, so she could leave that house. From the living room, she scolded her brother, yelling at him down the hallway.

"Hey!" she said. "Why can't you just walk into the house like a normal person?"

Jim came out of his room and looked at her. Rosa was struck by what she saw. His eyes appeared strange, the pupils dilated. She began to ask, "Have you been—" but he ignored her and left the house again.

"Great," she said. "Now there's something else we can't talk about."

Jim walked along their driveway toward the road. Soon, he spotted his Uncle Jefferson's blue Dodge parked alongside. Jim had telephoned and was eager to see a girl he was getting to know, Bethany Clark, who lived outside of town with his aunt and uncle.

"Hi, there, Jim!" His uncle waved to him from the car. "Sorry, but my wife and Beth are working late at the rest home," he said. "I don't know if you still want to come by, or not. The kids are doing something over at the school. It'd just be you and me."

"Uh, maybe another time," Jim said. "I still have things I need to do at home," which was a lie.

Jefferson rattled on, saying, "Gee, whiz. That's too bad. I was lookin' forward to some time together. You know me. I love having someone to talk to. Okay, so, maybe another time?"

"Sure."

Jim pretended to walk back to his house, waiting for his uncle to be out of sight. Once the car disappeared up Pine Way Junction, Jim turned around and hurried toward Sylvia's house.

A battle ensued between feeling guilty for having deceived his uncle and what was emerging from within himself. Life, it seemed to Jim, had become too complicated. Graduation loomed and, what he planned to do beyond his senior year, was yet unclear. Seeing his way through proved impossible.

Luckily, he thought, there was always Sylvia. He knew which window was her's and got her attention by tossing a stick into the air outside the window. He tried talking her into coming outside, "just for a little while," but she refused.

"I need to talk to you, Syl," he said.

"I can't, Jim. You have to leave."

"Is there someone else?" he asked.

"I'm not telling."

He knew it. "Who is it?"

"Nobody."

"C'mon. Just for a little while. I need to tell you something."

"Tell me now."

"No. I can't tell you here. It's—"

"I'm not going anywhere with you, Jim."

"Why not?"

"Because I said so." She slid the window shut.

The screen door opened and Sylvia's Aunt Justice stepped onto her front porch. Hands on hips and a glaring stare in her eyes, informed Jim he had better leave. Giving up, he wandered homeward. At the end of the street, he turned to look back, spotting Aunt Justice again. Flowery straw hat on head and purse in hand, she was briskly walking toward town. No matter. Jim no longer wanted to see Sylvia, or anyone. Fed-up, instead of going home, he hurried over to the creek that flowed alongside town at the mountain's feet. No destination in mind, he merely went where he longed to be, away.

He entered the woodland bordering the stream and noticed the racket of bird life in the trees. A small animal, maybe a squirrel, dashed through the weedy undergrowth. Herbaceous plants and shrubs withered beneath the summer sun, but not so under the shady canopy where he made his way toward the stream. Here, they were yet green and lush. Berry thickets hung heavy with ripe and sweetened fruit. Vines draped the tree trunks. He carefully stepped around stones, crunching tinder-dry grasses where his boots tread. His arms brushed against the shrubby plant life, which left their aromatic scent on his skin. The creek was so low, his shoes remained untouched by the water as he crossed to the other side.

After climbing the embankment, he discovered an old trail across Pine Way Junction, once known only to his mother's native ancestors. He followed it up the mountainside, leaving behind the slender-leaved willows and the cottonwoods, their leaves like shimmering medallions. He entered the forest where warm air carried the sweet scent of pine.

Pent-up emotions rose within himself and tears he hid beneath his anger began to flow. Believing he was alone, he cried freely, his chest burning. He was relieved to let go, to be himself. He shed the falseness, the phony football star and "cowboy," which flirtatious girls at school called him. Most people in town, he figured, saw him as "that crazy mental case," so, he let that go as well. He cried and yet felt stronger, more real. This truth he knew as he finally stopped walking and sat upon the pine needles beneath the trees.

Westward, he gazed, until his eyes rested upon the bucolic landscape of his birth. He saw the town that was his whole world he felt had betrayed him with its pretend pleasantries and meaningless expectations. Here, on the edge of everything, watching the sun lowering in the sky, the wind alighted like a great bird come upon him, its presence stirring in the pines. The exhilarating updraft was like a wave, as though a siren's form drew upon his soul. Within his grasp, the last rays of sunlight, like dusty beams of soft, golden air, and the trees, like tall sentinels paying homage to the land of his dreams, became beautiful and wondrous. He wanted to hold on to the experience. He wanted all that was real to fill him with each breath, until all that was false, in his thoughts and in his view, drained from him. The wind gusted momentarily, then settled into the darkening hills of evening's quiet. His breath calmed and he became still. Words came to him, which he spoke aloud.

"What does the world offer a man who looks upon thee? You are all I want. No one can claim me, but you. I belong to you, only you."

He sat for maybe an hour and, as soon as he decided to go home, he heard someone walking up the same path, hearing their labored breath. He became angry, not because he could be in danger, but because he wanted to be alone and had found a place where he could free his heart to run. Someone was coming, like everyone else, intruding on his privacy, crowding him. He thought he could simply walk away unseen. Maybe they would continue on by, he thought. But, once they came into view, he saw it was a woman and became curious.

She saw Jim and apologized, "I'm sorry to bother you. I'm just on my way up to Sister Ruth's. The retreat house?"

He remembered Walter Henry had said his sister, Lulabelle, changed her name to Sister Ruth. He realized the trail could be used by anyone who stayed with her.

"It's okay," he said. "I just came up here to get away for a bit."

"That's why I'm here," she said.

The woman stopped to catch her breath, then turned to watch the sunset. Its last departing rays disappeared along the mountain ridge in the west.

"It's so pretty," she said.

Her name was Katie. She had light-colored, maybe reddish-blond hair, and was dressed in pants with a man's shirt tucked in, and she wore canvas shoes. Jim never saw her before, but knew she was not one of the locals. She said goodbye and continued on her way through the woods. The sun had set and, with only his memory to guide him, he hiked the trail back down the mountain to home. He felt a soothing quietness within himself, a soft hush, as though a blanket of whispering gentleness filled him. Time alone in the woods gave him this needed sense of peace.

It became a regular habit for Jim to take long treks into the forest, an opportunity to see things he had no idea were in his own backyard. He startled a black bear lumbering along one time, sniffing the air as Jim approached it. His mother went for walks, but he never told her, or anyone, that he now ventured into the woods, himself. Rosa was always gone, it seemed to him. His mother worked long hours with the other farmworkers. When she was off work, she helped his grandma. His dad was hardly ever around. Jim cynically gave some thought to what his father could be doing besides work. "Probably with what's-her-name," he said aloud. Whatever the case, Jim was free to take his walks without question, without having to talk about it.

He thought about that woman he had seen, figured she was somewhere in her twenties. She dressed like a man. Her hair was extremely short. But, she was pretty, in a different sort of way, he thought. He was curious about a woman who did not bother to be appealing. Hoping to see her again, he was pleased when it happened. This time, it was he who intruded on her privacy.

He said, "Hi," and raised his hand to wave, then stopped to talk to her. "So, are you still staying at the retreat house?" he asked, pointing in that direction.

Katie smiled and said, "I'm still there. Not ready to leave." She assumed he thought as she did, that it was pretty pathetic to still be at a retreat center.

"I keep coming back up here," he said.

"It's nice and quiet," she told him, "not many people around, you know?"

"Yeah, I come up here to get away from all that," he said, hooking his thumb over his shoulder toward the town.

"Did you grow up here?" she asked.

Jim sat near Katie, drew his legs up and propped his arms across his knees. Looking out upon the woods, he said, "Yep. This is all I know." He picked up a small twig and proceeded to snap it to pieces. "Pine Way and Edenville," he added.

"Do you like it?" she asked.

He laughed a little, thinking, "hell, no!" But, then, he shrugged his shoulders and answered, "I never thought about it much, 'til I started comin' up here."

Katie listened to him, which encouraged him to open up to her. She was unlike Sylvia, and his mother, but, most of all, Beth. He saw something about her and knew she was like him, wounded and hurting deep inside, though there was something else he sensed, something that attracted him.

He looked toward the view of the valley and picked up another stick to occupy his fingers and said, "It's like—I grew up here, never thinking about whether I liked it or not, then things got really crazy and—" He paused, looking for the right words. "I don't know," he said and threw the stick down. "It's all mixed up. There's just too much to think about." He wanted to tell her how he felt, about which he had never told another. Trying, he said, "Everyone's like, do this, don't do that, go here, go there. School's gonna start and I'm supposed to be some football hero." He laughed and shook his head. "Shoot! I haven't even figured out who I am, I mean, not really." He swatted at a mosquito in its high, thin buzzing around his head.

"What are they saying you should do?" Katie asked.

"My teachers say I should go to college," Jim answered. "My old man wants me to take over the family business, but all I want is—"

He stopped, because he felt himself stepping into a place where he was afraid to go, a place of truth and terror, of beauty and ugliness. Looking at her sitting close by, he felt himself drawn to her, which terrified him. He shifted his body away and looked down at the ground, withdrawing into himself and, in his frustration, tore at a nearby plant.

"Are you okay?" she asked.

Katie had picked up on Jim's shift in mood. He seemed like a regular kid with regular kid problems, like school, peer pressure, and parents, until whatever it was came over him. He became very quiet, a brooding sort of quiet. She was uncertain whether he was safe to be alone with, so she decided to walk back to the retreat house, using that as her excuse.

"Well, I better be getting back," she said. "Sister Ruth's probably wondering what's taking me so long. I only meant to be gone a short while."

They both stood up and it was then that she knew why she felt unsafe with him. He was like her, having been hurt very badly by someone. In addition, he was not only handsome, but she found him very attractive, the way he moved, physical and...something else that appealed to her, a kinship, perhaps. She had to make herself turn away and leave, hastily saying goodbye and walking away. After several steps, she stopped and looked back at him, watching him walk down the mountain, her heart already missing him.

An unspoken arrangement led to continued meetings. Eventually, they acted on their sexual attraction for one another.

It was only a few times, because Jim's life became full again. Football practice geared up, then school, along with all the studying and homework and, of course, work with his father. He was so busy, he had no time to meet Katie. It scarcely mattered. She knew he was back in school and had, herself, left the retreat house for home. More at peace than when she had first arrived, she was also pregnant, which she did not discover for a month or two after she returned home.

CHAPTER FOURTEEN

Candelaria stood with rake in hand, helping to clean the horse stalls at the barn, when a woman showed up, looking for Jimmy.

"Is Jimmy around?" she asked.

Her blond hair was styled in the latest fashion. Candelaria found it unbelievable this woman had prettied herself with make-up for a trip to a horse barn. Her outfit was so tight, she knew that men would say something about brick outhouses once they got a load of her in her dark mustard-yellow jeans and matching chamois shirt. The woman even accessorized with a gold scarf and gold clip-on earrings.

Glancing over Candelaria's house dress and hair in a kerchief, the woman told her, "He promised to come by our ranch to take a look at my horse. She's been limping. I'm not sure if she needs shoeing, or what could be the trouble."

Trouble, was the word.

Dismissing the woman with an, "I don't know where he is," Candelaria charged off for home.

Jimmy was caught unaware when she descended upon the house.

"Some woman came into the barn looking for you!" she shouted from the living room.

Jimmy was busy making sandwiches in the kitchen. "Yeah? Who was it?" he asked.

Like a fiery tempest, Candelaria said, "How should I know?! I don't keep a list of your girlfriends!"

"Girlfriends?!" Jimmy went to the doorway of the kitchen to ask her, "What are you talking about?"

"It's obvious she wanted you to pay a special visit to her house, just to see her!"

Jimmy closed his eyes for a moment, shaking his head, already disgusted with his wife. "Oh, good gawd, Larie," he said. "Don't start on that, would you please?"

"I will start on it until it comes to a stop! I'm sick of your fooling around with these other women!"

Jimmy's eyes glazed over as his heart shut down. Out of sheer survival, he left the house and returned to work, regardless of whether that woman was still at the livery stable. His only need was to go.

Candelaria remained standing in the living room. Still angry, she folded her arms in front of herself and fumed. Checking to see what her husband was doing in the kitchen, she spotted a loaf of bread and a canned ham on the table beside their picnic basket. Seeing the contents of the basket, it dawned on her that he was making them a picnic lunch, that he was trying. Her anger gave way to that familiar, yet tiresome remorse she knew well. All she could do was sit at the table and bury her head in her arms, sobbing one more time for what she knew not how to repair.

• • •

Jimmy's reputation with women may have dimmed over the years since he and Candelaria married, but she was continually faced with the obvious. The flame had not gone out entirely. Lonely ranch women, living in isolated areas on their sprawling horse properties, occasionally flirting behind their husband's back, was one thing, she thought. But, there was one woman who presented a definite threat.

Her name was Joan. Her last name never mattered to Candelaria. Joan worked in the office at the racehorse stables where Jimmy often assisted their resident, salaried farrier. The only reason he was getting work there so frequently, was because of Joan's devious manipulations to bring him to her. She had plans, designs, and outright competitive drive. Candelaria, the wife who helplessly stood by, was forced to take action.

The confrontation took place when the children were yet little. Joan had tried to win Candelaria's daughter's affections, offering to take the girl shopping in town, commenting on, "Rosalita, wouldn't you rather wear dresses? Why, I know of the most darling little dress shop where you and I would have so much fun. Hmm? What do you say?"

She stroked Rosalita's hair before the girl scurried off as fast as her nearly thirteen-year-old, long, skinny legs could take her directly to her mother.

"She's creepy, Mom! You've got to do something! She's got Daddy wrapped around her finger like he was her husband, not yours!"

That did it. Candelaria had not accompanied her husband only to be ignored and disrespected both by him and by Joan What's-Her-Name. She told her daughter to "watch and learn," then walked into Joan's office and pounced on the woman with all her fury.

"How dare you try to wheedle your serpentine clutches into my family!" she said. "It's bad enough you throw yourself shamelessly at my husband, making a fool of yourself, but then trying to insert yourself into my daughter's life behind my back is the lowest!"

She placed her hands on top of the desk and leaned toward Joan What's-Her-Name cringing behind it. Looking directly into the woman's eyes, she said, "Don't you ever so much as look at my children ever again!" Candelaria's voice lowered but did not lose its power as she said, "As for my husband, he's got a mind of his own, but, between you and me, if I ever witness or so much as hear of you trying anything with my husband, I'll—" She could not bring herself to threaten murder, so she said, "I'll see to it your scandalous, scheming, slutty reputation gets spread all across this county!"

Candelaria then strode out of the office and to her daughter's side.

"How's that?" she asked.

"That was great, Mom! You were super!"

Jimmy came walking around the corner of the building. "Time to call it a day," he said. Looking at them, he asked, "What?"

Candelaria and her daughter looked at one another and laughed. Chiming in together, they said, "Oh, nothing!"

Candelaria never knew if her words had any effect on Joan What's-Her-Name's ambitions, but she planned to not go there anymore. Since she lost her babies, she had enough cleaning up after and taking care of horses that belonged to other people, particularly other women. Since that confrontation took place, she decided she had enough of Jimmy's games as well. Candelaria was moving on.

Joan evidently had a change of heart the day Jimmy was killed in a tragic and violent accident. She shed no tears for him, which surprised herself, most of all. She cried in guilt and anguish for

Candelaria, always knowing Jimmy truly loved his wife. When Candelaria cried in her shock and grief as her husband's broken body was carried away on a stretcher, Joan instinctively placed an arm around her. Holding her and lending her strength, she said in a soft voice, only to Candelaria, "I'm sorry, Larie. I'm so sorry."

She truly meant it, apologizing not only for her scheming ways, but for Candelaria's impending loss, the love of her life, that no one, not even Joan could steal away.

Too distraught, Candelaria was unaware of Joan's act of kindness that day. On the contrary, she would always remember the experience as the strength of angels bearing her up when the ambulance arrived and then drove away, taking her love and her life with them.

CHAPTER FIFTEEN

The funeral was over and the gathering of family and friends at the Hart's home had dispersed. Ev and a few other ladies helped Candelaria clean, so she could lie down and rest. Rosa came out of her room and joined them. Jim slipped away to his own room, wanting to be alone. Once he closed the door, the loss of his father seized upon his soul like a heavy embrace, cloaking his inner being in frightening sorrow.

Before his father's accident, Jim had begun cleaning out his room, excitedly preparing to go away, to begin training for his first season playing college football. But, his room had changed, becoming meaningless as though it belonged to someone else. The bed was not his, nor the small desk and metal office lamp. A small dresser by the closet with a broken drawer and missing knobs was not his dresser. The few pictures torn from magazines and tacked to the wall, he ripped away and left them where they fell to the floor. What was once so necessary, his team jacket, his football jerseys, and cleats were shoved into a box. He carried it to the barn, planning to add it to the dust-enshrouded piles of the past accumulating in one corner.

The blacksmith shop was still. The midday sun shone through the doorway and across the barn floor. One horse whinnied to Jim when he entered the livery stable. He set the box on the workbench and approached the animal. Drawing its head down nearer to his own, he sheltered his grief there in quiet gasps while smoothing its soft coat with his hands.

Jim had grown since the previous summer, reaching nearly six feet tall. Although athletic and muscular, he had yet to develop the bulkiness of the older man he would become. His skin was only noticeably brown, but had an olive tinge from his Spanish roots, his features fine, unlike his mother's. She showed more of her native ancestry in her facial features and had thick hair. His was not a large-boned frame, but not delicate like his sister's, whose physical features also showed her Spanish blood. Whereas Rosa had her own unique temperament, Jim's was identical to his mother's as though drawn from the same well. Springing forth from deep within bedrock, their moods brewed where the earth's molten core lay hid. His father's influence would come forward more as he got older, though the connection to his mother would remain.

His brown, curly-wavy hair had been cut short for graduation. He wore brown slacks, a cream-colored shirt and brown jacket, and a yellow-gold tie his Grandma Ev had given him. The suit he bought himself, even the shoes. The tie clip was his father's. Jim often pictured himself wearing his new brown suit when he left town to go out into the world, though never to attend his father's funeral.

The last time he saw his father, he was standing outside the barn. Recalling that day, his fingers rubbed the gold horseshoe on the tie clip, which had his father's birthstone imbedded in it. It was also Jim's birthstone, for they shared the same birth month. His mother was having fun, carrying their lunch she had packed in a basket, her hair in a ponytail, like a teenager. Jim remembered noticing she was behaving girlish, and cherished the memory, for it was part of the last goodbye.

"Well, I guess we're off!" his father said.

Jimmy sat in the truck, looking at his son and Walter Henry standing side by side like glum hound dogs, before turning his head to bicker playfully with his wife.

"Good grief, Larie. You'd think we were goin' on a big vacation, or somethin'!" he said.

She asked him, "What do you mean?"

"I mean, what is all this stuff?" Jimmy answered.

Winking at his son and grinning, Jimmy shot his hand out the truck window to signal his farewell before he and his wife drove away.

Later that day, a call came in at the post office, the postmaster running to the blacksmith shop to tell Walter Henry that another one of the Hart men was near death. Jimmy Hart was trampled viciously by a killer stallion, he reported. The old blacksmith dreaded telling Jim, but hated to hold such terrible news on his mind. Another father killed and Walter Henry felt himself buckle under the weight of its awfulness. Like a dark tremor, a convulsive shock wave, the news overwhelmed him and he cried in agony.

Jim ran to him, worried the man had burned himself at the forge.

"Somethin' happened to your dad," said Walter Henry. "Go get your sister and your grandmother."

Jim stood there in shock, the information not registering.

"I said, go," the old man tried to shout.

Jim took Walter Henry's truck and drove to his grandmother's, then went to the beauty parlor to pick up Rosa. Patience McGrew, Dottie, and Mary Stewart closed up the beauty parlor and followed behind in Patty's car. His Grandma Ev was praying under her breath, like murmuring whispers, seated beside him in the truck with her eyes closed. Jim merely stared out the windshield, acting mechanically to drive here, drive there, drive back.

The postmaster, Geoffrey Cadwallader, who was Robert's brother and Sylvia's uncle, called the infirmary to get a doctor to come out and help Walter Henry. Jefferson Hart and his wife left work right away, following the doctor's car to the livery stable. Beth rode with them. Once they arrived, she ran to Jim, knowing then that she loved him. Her heart sought out his, to comfort him and to be held by him in return.

"Jim!" she cried.

He hurried to meet her. They held one another as he brought her into the barn, where others had gathered around Walter Henry. He was seated on a bale of hay, leaning against one of the stalls. He had suffered a heart attack. Someone brought him water. Everyone else stood around and waited. Patrons from the ·post office stood out front of the building, watching the commotion, discussing amongst themselves what was taking place. The sculptor, Tommy McGrew, who was Daddy McGrew's nephew and Dottie's cousin, came out of the old store to inquire after his friend. The newspaperman, Tucker Howard Stewart, who had taken over the paper with his son, Tucker James, stood outside their office, having heard the news. They were worried, also waiting and watching.

The phone rang again at the post office. Geoffrey Cadwallader went leaping and bounding, wide-eyed and bespectacled, to his neglected post, where it was confirmed that Jimmy Hart was dead. His body was taken from the hospital and delivered to the county morgue. Someone was driving his truck, bringing Candelaria back to Pine Way.

When she arrived, it was night. The townspeople had gathered together at the barn. They watched as she was aided out of the truck. She was awestruck by the scene before her, seeing the faces of all those who were once the children of The Way. Hart, Henry, McGrew, Cadwallader, Stewart, Walker, and Mendoza, they became like ghosts reborn, ancestors rising up once again. Though it was dark and the barn's outdoor light and the lantern which shone within were dim, she could see they were all anxious and expectant, worried and heartbroken. She and her children held one another and cried for yet another loss, another hole in their hearts to mend.

● ● ●

Jim's plan to leave home was not so important anymore. It became like all things the flood sweeps away once the waters overflow the banks of their keep. Giving the horse a final pat on its neck, he left its side to saunter toward the doorway. Hesitating, he turned to glance around the barn, so familiar, yet somehow more expansive, as if it had grown taller, wider. He noticed things he had not noticed before, a family of barn owls perched in the rafters, a heavy chain with a large hook attached, and a pulley hanging from a main crossbeam, the work bench, the vice...and rolls of baling wire from hay purchased...

Staring at the wire stacked beside the work bench, he grasped his arm and his scars became inflamed with memory. Like a flash, it came to him, the man's coarse voice, his brutish hands gripping him, keeping him from his mother. Her screams expelled from within her as though she were gasping for life. She lashed out at Mean Uncle right as the big man pushed Jim into the stack of baling wire, a sharp end raking the length of his arm.

With a roaring cry, Jim kicked at the pile. "Why do we keep all this sh—?!" he asked. Seeing the stacks of clutter in the corner of the barn, a fury rose from within, his breath as one climbing a steep mountain, determined to reach its summit before the storm arrived. With that single cry, came the knowledge of what he must do. He ran home to change out of his suit and into work clothes and boots, then hurried back to the barn, returning to something that was his. His mother told him so. Walter Henry had shook his hand and called him, "partner."

He got the truck and backed it up to the doorway, parked, then began tossing the old piles of junk into the truck bed. The first thing that went were the coils of old baling wire, some so rusted, it seemed they would snap like a twig. He knew what they used and what they kept for just-in-case. All the rest was junk, like an old desk, stacks of horsemen's magazines, old tractor parts, the back seat of a car they no longer owned, rusted and useless odds and ends. All of it and more got tossed or dragged and hefted onto the truck bed. It took three trips to the dump before the corner of forgotten past lives was cleared away. He raked and spread fresh hay in the stable, raked the entire barn, and swept away cobwebs. What was lying on the ground found a new home on a hook or a nail. He worked until late, the lantern lit to help him see his way.

Exhausted, one gloved hand on his hip, the other sweeping his hair aside from his sweaty brow, he surveyed what he had accomplished. Pleased, eyes looking up and around the barn, it now appeared hopeful to him, and promising.

Softly, yet with strength, he said, "This is mine now. Mine and Walter's."

He looked up again into the rafters as, one by one, each of the barn owls silently took flight into the night sky. He heard their piercing screeches and knew he was done for the day. The following day, he would arise and go to work, with Walter Henry joining him after his recovery. Jim felt his purpose renewed even as his dream of leaving home was going unfulfilled.

"There's still time," he reassured himself. "There's still time."

CHAPTER SIXTEEN

Jim left the house with his shadow so close, it likely adhered itself to his back. He could not escape it. What lived within himself clung to the fabric of his soul, reaching and grasping, like the paws of some great animal fighting to be free. Eyes squinting, he looked high into the sky and all around at the forest that surrounded his home. The wind was blowing, sending leaves scattering and swirling down from the elm trees.

Months had passed since his father's death. He married his girlfriend, Bethany Clark, who stayed behind at the house while he stepped out for a walk. She was moving in, since his mother and Rosa packed up and left that morning. He knew he needed to keep his time away brief, so he could return to help her.

Pausing along the way, he turned to look back at the house, shocked to find it had strangely altered. The same building in which his family had made their home for most of his life, appeared unfamiliar to him. It were as though years spent away had passed and, upon his return, what he once knew and how he once felt, had disappeared, having slipped away. He fixated on this before continuing on his walk. The change in the house no longer his home, was held in its siding. Though he had always imagined a light-green house, he, only then, beheld a white house, scraped to bare wood in places. What happened to the dog he used to have? Curly. Where was the garden that lay withering into weeds? The arbor at the beginning of the path that led toward the porch was gone. The boy he was, who became a man, had left him. Or, had he left the boy? The dirt driveway, its furrowed paths that led toward or away from their home, were once so familiar for each stone and puddled depression he had memorized. But, it no longer went to his home. It went to a house belonging to someone he scarcely knew. Briefly disoriented, he left the scene behind and, like a mantle, draped his shadow and his anger close once more as he walked further along the woodland trail.

His stream of thoughts moved along, mulling over his anger and something in particular with which he had not yet come to terms: Katie's departure. At the first thought of her, it dawned on him that he had made a terrible mistake. Marrying Beth curtailed any chance he might have had with Katie. Although, he reminded himself, she disappeared from his life at summer's end the year before, though it felt like several. He wondered how he could yet love her and seek to dwell upon her memory while marrying Beth, whom he knew he cared for, though loved differently. His love for Katie, he knew, was in his best nature, his youthful, wild heart freed to be his true self that he treasured and had revealed to no one else.

He stopped to gaze into the treetops. The wind caused the fir and pine to sway slowly, gently, calming him. The view of his house returned to mind, summoning his grief to rise. His father's memory yet too raw, he continued through the woods, his pace quickening. Fear gripped him and he became like helpless prey in a darkened wood. He tried to ignore it stalking him, but something more was lost than a woman he knew one, brief summer and a father from whom he had become alienated. This realization captured his soul and tore him down. The words in anger he frequently spoke to his father, the loss of Katie, not knowing where she lived or how to find her, assailed him with regret. He hated himself for this betrayal he had inflicted upon his heart. He loved his father. He loved Katie. His true self he barely got to know, wanted her in his life, but he had married Beth. For that, he hated himself most of all.

He lost his way, but cared less as he wandered aimlessly between the trees. Beneath the palms of his hands, he felt their rough and scaly bark and stirred the scent of their needles when he brushed between the low branches. Deep down, the well stirred, its surface water rippling as a small pebble was dropped. Sylvia. He remembered their first night together, when his parents had gone to the meeting at school and Rosa went to a friend's house. He was supposed to be doing homework, but had preplanned with Sylvia to come over at a certain time. When she arrived, they were excited to be alone and were kissing and laughing in their sneaky, behind-the-back thrill. He took her to his room and, like they had planned, they slowly became each other's "first." Sylvia was only thirteen and in the eighth grade. Jim was fifteen, in his sophomore year of high school. Their excitement was intensified by the forbidden, secret nature of their adolescent tryst. Afterward, they lay together under the covers. Sylvia smiled, then laughed, and Jim kissed her. He drew her close to him. "I love you," he told her, but all she said was, "what's all that on your arm?"

With more of the memory surfacing from out of the shadows, Jim strode through the woods, the shade likewise deepening. He walked through his grandparent's abandoned fruit orchard behind their house, apples brown and shriveled on the stems. A deer, startled by his presence, bounded away through the trees. The grass and shrubs had grown tall in the neglected grove, dampening his clothes. He continued walking, until he neared the old picnic grounds where only trees and a hushed atmosphere could be found. He paused, remembering that he had first wanted to marry Sylvia, but it was impermissible. He pondered why, but the sly fox within himself, passing silently alongside, knew that Tucker Stewart probably asked himself the same thing. The girls they fought over, but it was Forty who got the girl they all loved. He and Beth. He asked himself how it happened. Forty and Sylvia. Jim began seething with anger and jealousy. Sylvia was his love, his girl. Katie came to mind again, but he dismissed that thought, because Katie was gone and what they had was but "a summer romance," he cynically concluded.

Walking further, he came upon the area where his little brothers were buried, their tiny, white quartz headstones only large enough for their names. Movement caught his eye. It was his mother. She was visiting her babies' long-rotted bones, where only a crucifix remained in each of the graves to protect them on their journeys. He turned to go, so as not to disturb her, but she spotted him and froze, a surprised look on her face, as though caught in something private, not for him to see.

"What are you doing here?!" she shouted at him, angrily. "I came here to be alone!"

"Okay! Okay! I'm going!" he said.

He turned away from her and walked quickly toward Pine Way Junction. No Sylvia, no life out in the world and, apparently, while he was choking on the bitter taste of his self-pity, no family, either. His father was dead. The unfamiliarity of their weather-worn house reminded him of that fact. His mother and Rosa had moved into the farmworkers housing. Plans to leave home and go away to college on a football scholarship had disappeared into nothingness, for they were lost, now belonging to the boy he left behind.

Remembrances continued of their own accord, returning to a specific day. The first time he told Sylvia that he loved her was supposed to be a special time for them. Even though Rosa reassured him, in the awful aftermath of that night, that she would tell no one what she saw, the memory of it was no less traumatic.

Rosa had arrived home early from her friend's house and heard voices coming from Jim's room. Curious, and giving it little forethought, she opened the door wide, walking in on them.

"Who's here?" she asked.

Sylvia pulled the blankets up to her chin. Rosa quickly scanned the room to see their clothes strewn across the floor.

Jim yelled at her, "Get the fu— out of here! Close the door!"

Rosa did, but was aghast at what she had seen and knew had happened. She escaped to the living room, shaking, arms folded in front of her and one hand rubbing her forehead, not knowing what to do. She went outside to wait for her parents to get home from the meeting at school.

A door slammed in the house. Jim shouted, "Sylvia! Don't go!"

Sylvia did go, hurrying away from their house and willingly entering the dark of night. Once absorbed into its seeming oblivion, she was blinded to the sight of Jim's parents on their way home.

Through the gaping front door, Rosa looked over her shoulder into the house, dreading a confrontation with her brother. She saw Jim in the kitchen frantically rummaging through the drawers, with utensils spilling and clanging onto the floor. He was looking for something sharp that, once found, became a weapon he proceeded to use on himself.

Rosa dashed into the kitchen to stop him, yelling, "No! No! Jim!"

It was too late. He had slashed a three-inch-long cut on the inside of his forearm.

"Why'd you do it, Jim?! Why?! Oh, God!"

•　　•　　•

The memory of Rosa's words faded from his mind as Jim approached the livery stable. Pacing in front of the barn, he debated whether to go inside or head for home, like he had promised Beth. She needed his help, she said. But, once opened, the door to his downfall began pulling him under and, unprepared for its force, his mind sank into a disturbed reality.

He believed he was unwanted by his own family. He was not to blame, he reminded himself. His father's death was not his fault. They were not his actions that brought distance into the family. He would never wish his troubles onto them.

A build-up of emotion overwhelmed Jim until it seemed like the family's problems were his fault. Without thinking, he unlocked the door to the barn, remembering that day again, Rosa catching him and Sylvia in bed together and Sylvia angry with him for humiliating her as she said, "Now everyone will think I'm a—

"No, they won't!" Jim shouted. "Rosa won't tell anybody!"

Jim was trying to get Sylvia to calm down and stay, but she left and Jim's fears took over. In his panic, he fell away as the walls breathed in upon him. He feared losing her and he feared remembering Mean Uncle, who prevented his mother from protecting him. His mother was unable to stop the torment. That was all Jim had ever known and wanted to be made unknown. The words of Jackson penetrated all reasoning. The dark poison, the sinister intent of his words worked on him as Jim entered the barn.

"You're just a throwback," said Mean Uncle. "Anybody can see that. Your mother doesn't even want you."

Jim opened the barn door and entered a shadowy place, fearing the veracity of his uncle's words. Rosa was the only child his mother wanted, he thought. Considering his brothers she now grieved, he asked, "Would she miss me, if I died, too?" The thought came to him that the only way he could get his mother to want him again, was to die as well. "Then, she'll want me," he said. "If I die, she'll want me."

He climbed up to the loft and, laying himself down upon piles of hay, began imagining what it would be like to die. Would he simply disappear from life? he asked himself. Or, would he pass between worlds, knowing both at the same time? What was death to him, except where his father had gone and his baby brothers? He knew, in a way, they were not dead, but had passed on, moved on to some place where he was not allowed to follow until his own time arrived. It was a mystery to him, death. The life that came after, he knew, was as real as this life he yet lived. His father was no longer at their house. He was not in the barn. Jim imagined his father was with his mother, visiting the old graves with her, comforting her.

Jim looked around the barn from where he lay, noticing its weathered boards and creaking frame that threatened to collapse with the next gust of wind. He fell asleep and dreamed of his father. The dream appeared as peculiar as the fate of their old house. He left the barn and was walking past Pine Way, his father walking on the dirt road ahead of him. Excited to see him, Jim hurried to catch up, calling out, "Dad!" He tried to reach him, but his father kept walking steadily away, his momentum as one conveyed along a road spanning far into another reality. Jim stopped and remained in place, watching his father walk away until it seemed the man had become a stranger, too. A mystery.

A last flurry of bird song in the trees was all Jim heard when he awoke. The sun had set and the day at last came to its resting place, waiting for its own death, he mused. By the time he climbed down from the loft, he was calm, subdued. After making sure all was well inside the barn, he said good night to the lone horse in its stall, slid the back barn door on its track until it was closed, and bolted it. He went out the front and closed the wide doors and padlocked them, then walked home on the path through the trees he knew so well, for every dip and bump, and every tree root memorized.

Beth was at home. Her car, an old one given her by Jefferson and his wife, was parked out front. Jim went up the steps and into the house, no cowboy hat on his head, for he had left it somewhere. He slipped off his boots and set them by the door. Beth was singing while she cleaned and rearranged the furniture to her own taste. Jim was glad. He was glad she was there, thankful that at least she stood by him. The other women in his life had left him, but Beth had not. She chose to be with him, to love him no matter what, no matter the scars on his arms, no matter what lived within him and wrestled to be free. He went to her and held her, so earthy in her womanly touch, her full and rounded plumpness, so ready and willing to please him, to be his.

"My wife." He kissed her, then lifted her into his arms. "All that cleaning can wait," he told her. He carried her into the bedroom, where the bed would be unmade and remain that way for a long time as he loved her and filled her with his life.

CHAPTER SEVENTEEN

Anxiety, depression, and an inability to keep a job, used to be minor setbacks for Jim's old girlfriend, Katie. She tried to care for their baby, but had too many problems. Sleeping on her friend's couch and borrowing money, old habits of her's, produced an unstable life for raising a child.

Her mother refused to help her, saying, "It's your own fault for gettin' into that mess!" She fought with Katie about bringing "it" into the house, referring to the baby, even threatened to report her own daughter to the authorities.

Desperate and agonizing over what to do, Katie fled back to Edenville, the one place where she had known love and security. She remembered where Jim worked, a safer place to see him than at his house, she thought. Inquiring about him at the drug store, the cashier whispered the news that Jim had gotten married. Grateful for the information, Katie thanked the cashier and left the store.

Seated, with the car door wide open, she had second thoughts about trying to see Jim. It had never occurred to her that he would marry, and at so young an age. Nevertheless, she followed the directions out to the Pine Way end of town and parked at the livery stable. Hesitant whether to get out of the car, she needed only to recall her mother's threat to prompt her into action.

"You've got no place here in my house anymore," her mother said. "You ought to be ashamed of yourself! I'll report you to the authorities, is what I'll do if you don't leave!"

Katie's choice was made. She needed to find someone to take care of her boy, someone she could trust who would keep him safe. Gathering what courage she had, she carried her son toward the open doorway of the barn. Walter Henry greeted her. Recognizing him immediately as Sister Ruth's brother, she became hopeful.

"Where's Jim?" she asked in a worried tone.

Walter Henry looked over the young woman standing before him. Not much bigger than a boy, and dressed like one, too, he judged.

"What do you want with Jim?" he asked. Once the question was out, he knew the answer.

In her haste, Katie stepped forward and gave him the child. "He's gonna be two on the fourth, month after next," she said. Returning to the car to retrieve a few small bundles, she then handed him a bag of toys, some diapers, and clothes, and said, "His name's Johnny. Jim's the father, but I've been telling people only my last name, so—"

His arms full, Walter Henry began to protest.

Katie became upset and cried out, "I've got no place to go! I can't take care of a child! My mother's talkin' like she'll report me to the authorities and he'll be taken from me! I know Jim wouldn't want that!" She was near hysterics, but calmed down and said, "Please, you've got to help me. Sister Ruth was so kind. She took me in when I had no one else to turn to."

Walter Henry was surprised to hear her mention his sister's name. He knew his sister would want him to help the young woman, even if it meant keeping the child.

He weakly nodded his head and, barely audible, said, "Okay."

Sad and dejected, the last thing Katie said was, "Jim was real nice to me. He was a good friend."

Shaking and nearly exhausted from the ordeal, she got in her car and drove off, uncertain as to the fate of her son.

Walter Henry wondered how a woman could leave her child like that, muttering, "She probably cut the cord, herself."

The boy giggled and pulled on Walter Henry's nose. The blacksmith realized that, as old as he was, he had become a father, too. He looked at the little boy in his arms, hair the color of dried cornhusks, and fell in love.

He said to Johnny, "You're a lot of trouble, you know that?"

He set the bundles down on the workbench and smiled in adoration of the child he held in his arms. Johnny yanked on the brim of his hat, then rested his head on Walter Henry's shoulder. The gruff oldster's heart was won.

"You sure about this?" he asked. "I'm an old geezer, pretty set in my ways."

He hugged the boy no one wanted, was how he saw it. But, he wanted Johnny. "Yeah, I guess you can stay," he said.

Jim was coming up the path from his house, something Walter Henry had seen the young man do when he was a boy like the one Walter Henry held in his arms. He had seen Jim's father walk up that path when only a boy, too.

"Well," he told himself aloud, "I better stop thinkin' like that. I'm starting to feel old."

When Jim reached the barn, he smiled and asked, "Who's this?"

"This is Johnny." Still feeling special, Walter Henry grinned.

"Johnny? You didn't tell me you had a kid, Walt," teasing his partner.

"Oh, he ain't mine."

Walter Henry knew he should at least say, "he's yours," if only to see the expression on Jim's face. But, in the moment, he decided not to do that. He would have to lie.

"Well, this cousin of mine came by, got herself into trouble, asked for my help. I said I'd do it." The old blacksmith grinned again, pleased with himself, because it was only partly a lie.

Jim was suspicious, wondering about something and not completely believing Walter Henry's story. Nevertheless, he played along.

When Walter Henry arrived home from work that day with a toddler in his arms, Sister Ruth called him over to her cabin. Without going into any details, she told her brother that Katie stopped by and informed her of what took place. They discussed the matter and agreed to raise the boy, giving him the Henry name. If someone inquired about Johnny, they would stick to their story, never mind if anyone believed it.

Sister Ruth's only opinion in the matter was voiced at that time and never again. "I've offered to help Jim more than once," she said. "I feel so sorry for him. But, he gets that old sourpuss face of his and acts like he doesn't know what I'm talkin' about."

She was much older than her brother, her years beginning to show in white hair and an easier heart that felt the whole world's pain. So, when she said, "He's got a wild soul, that man," she said it through weepy old eyes. Her last words in the matter were, "I'm afraid Johnny won't be safe livin' with him."

It was then that she and Walter Henry decided Jim must not be told the truth. Therefore, they found it necessary to keep the knowledge of Johnny's paternity from Jim's wife, Beth, and Jim's mother and sister.

Believing it was for the best to be Johnny's sole guardians without any fuss or complications from Jim's family, Walter Henry concluded the matter by saying, "We've got a responsibility to Johnny's mother first. I've given her my word we'd help her out."

Sister Ruth was pleased, especially since she knew Katie's plan to live close by and somehow remain in Johnny's life. Sworn to secrecy, the old woman of the mountain would never reveal Katie's secret, not to the law and not to her brother, Walter Henry.

* * *

It was difficult having a small child at the barn. Nevertheless, Jim and Walter Henry soon fell into a routine, something the old blacksmith knew how to do after three generations of Hart families being raised around horses. Jim found some old things from his and his sister's babyhood days at the house, but what Johnny loved the best were those Walter Henry made, some toys, a little chair and table, and a few carved animals. Taking care of the boy together felt right. The same way Jim's grandfather, Timothy Hart, became like a big brother to Walter Henry long ago, Walter Henry stepped in to support Jim, when Jim had lost his father. With Johnny there, it made sense to continue to help each other out.

Somewhere through the years, the two families, Hart and Henry, had bonded. For, that is what the Hart's and the Henry's were, family. Walter Henry got a bit teary-eyed one day at the realization, saying to himself, "By golly, me and Johnny are related." When he tried to figure it out, he stopped, fearing it would turn out to be one of those conundrums, like Johnny being his first cousin, so many times removed, or some such nonsense. He chuckled at the thought, saying, "Johnny may be a Henry, after all," and laughed out loud at the discovery. "Well, doggone it," he realized, "Jim and I are cousins, too." He decided to end this line of thinking. Not only did it worry him, it got him all mixed up in the head. He left it at the fact that his Aunt Rebecca Henry was Johnny's great-great-grandmother, so Johnny was a Henry, too, period.

However, it became worrisome when Johnny reached the same age as Jim was when Mean Uncle Jackson abused him. The old blacksmith was reminded of this and alerted to the danger into which Johnny was placed. He saw Jim nervously scratching at his arm, blood soaking through his shirt sleeve. Jim always wore long-sleeved shirts to hide his scars, even on the hottest days. Johnny was on the ground near the doorway of the barn, quietly playing with the toys Walter Henry had made. Jim was frozen to the spot, staring at the child and picking at his arm. Snapping out of it, he looked at his sleeve and hurried off for home.

Walter Henry followed him, calling out his name, "Jim!"

Jim stopped and looked behind him, a wild fear in his eyes.

Not knowing what to say, the old man simply grabbed ahold of Jim and held him in his arms as Jim began to sob loudly.

"I gotcha, Son. I gotcha," said Walter Henry.

Jim calmed down and returned to the barn to bandage himself, then rinsed the blood out of his shirt. Walter Henry never offered to help and was never asked. He took Johnny away from the barn and went home. From that day forward, he began to see another change in Jim's behavior, for the worse. He knew he was going to have to restrict the amount of time the boy spent in his father's presence, leaving the old man with a pain in his heart he knew not how to resolve.

CHAPTER EIGHTEEN

By the time Johnny appeared in their lives, Beth Hart had become a heavy drinker, sometimes leaving work early so she could get home to start in. Suspicions festered in her mind like an angry wound, when she saw Johnny with Jim and the old blacksmith in front of the hardware store one day. When she lived with Jim's Uncle Jefferson, she overheard him mentioning to his wife about what he had seen on more than one occasion one summer. Beth remembered specifically it was before their senior year.

Edenville was a small town and no one, not anyone, got away with anything for long. It was that way with Jim Hart and Katie. He was seen walking the trail, going up the hillside on the outskirts of town, "with some woman," Jefferson said. Lowering his emphatic ramblings down a notch, when his wife put her finger to her lips to shush him, he whispered a bit too loudly, "They were walking *together!*"

Jefferson had confronted Jim about it, reminding him that Beth was under their guardianship until she was eighteen and they did not want her to get hurt. "You watch your p's and q's, young man," he warned Jim. He later told his wife, "Jim is seeing that woman." In his outrage, he made his point, wagging his head as he circled their kitchen, repeating, "He didn't deny it. He didn't deny it."

The revelation made an impression on Beth back in their high school days, before she began dating Jim, when she had hopes. Seated on the sofa, looking out the front window, she rolled her eyes in regret and horror that this was the reasoning she had applied in agreeing to go out with Tucker Stewart. She had to admit, it got her the results she wanted. Jim took her seriously after that. To see him with that boy, calculating his age, if he was born the following year before they graduated from high school, she knew in all seriousness that she was a fool.

Her obsessing ate at her. She poured herself another drink and said, "That's Jim's son. I know it is," and dinner was forgotten.

Though Johnny favored his mother's looks, some aspects to his physical characteristics and behavior were identical to Jim's. The shape of his head, his facial features, and even the way he smiled told everyone in town the truth.

"More fodder for the gossipers in town," Walter Henry said. "I swear, they have no other joy in life than to talk about everybody else."

Jefferson Hart, one of the most talkative persons in town fit into that category. Gossip was craftily woven into his long-winded monologues Beth heard as they worked together. He was a tall, skinny man with graying, ashen-brown hair and a mustache. His white apron, by the end of the shift, was as greasy as his usage of the English language when it came to talking about other people. On he would go, one subject leading him into the next.

"I tell you, I think ol' Bobby Cadwallader is about ready to check himself in. Boy, he sure turned out to be a lush. Might as well camp out at Klucky's! He spends more time there than anywhere else. Maybe he's trying to win the biggest drinker award!" Scraping the grill with a spatula and stirring around the bacon frying, he would start in on the next person. "Speaking of awards," he said, "my kid got cheated out of—"

Jefferson's voice faded into the background of her thoughts as Beth's heart drowned in sorrow and anger, and glassfuls of whiskey. Nevertheless, she pressed the painful subject of Johnny's paternity. She believed she had won Jim from that woman he was seeing, that he chose her over his summer fling. When they walked together between classes in the school's corridors, second semester of their senior year, she felt triumphant, his arm about her waist. She had even won him from all the girls who swooned over him at school. The new boy in town proved her wrong. Beth knew they were close, her husband and that cute little boy, a son which she, herself, could not give Jim.

She had assumed it was her husband, the reason they were unable to have children. When she saw Jim with that boy, she knew the truth. She was not Jim's first pick, or his first love. That had been, "Little Miss Sylvia." Nor was she his second pick. That was the boy's mother. Miserable and heartbroken, Beth sank under the weight of her drunken rationale she mistook for the truth. In her mind, she was the one Jim was forced to settle for, because he could not have the one he wanted, nor the one he was too young for, who had made him a father. The way she saw it, she was the only one he could claim, because she was the only one who chose him and stood by him.

Glass in hand, she said, "I'm not so drunk I can't see that I've kept Jim from pursuing his dream," and downed the last drop. She never forgot his goal to leave town after graduation, a goal which never included her, she believed.

Their marriage was fine, at first. In fact, it was glorious. They finally gave in to their mutual feelings for one another. Beth was ready for marriage, ready and willing to be his wife and the mother of his children, like all the wives of the Hart men in the past. First one year, then two years, then more went by, and no pregnancy. Not because they were shy about it, either. Their bed never got made, since it would only get unmade, so she let it go. Come to think of it, while she was dredging her self-esteem through the dirt of her shortcomings, she neglected a lot of the household duties. Feeling remorse for her slovenly ways, she realized she never made an effort or had an interest in going to the livery stable or in riding horses with Jim, something he loved and in which he took great pride. All they had in common when they married was their desire to have a family and drinking.

"That boy," Beth further ruminated in her lowly, swilling agony, "was born the year we were married."

Her husband and the whole town, she believed, knew she could not give Jim a child, but that other woman had. However, an idea came to Beth, about which she secretly reveled. She could still hold her head up in town, because Jim could not openly claim the boy as his. Johnny Henry, she reassured herself, determined to have some satisfaction, would never become Johnny Hart.

Walter Henry was not so naive as to believe no one suspected or outright knew the truth. Yet, in all his years living in that speck on the county map, he had come to know its forgiving and accepting nature. If he said Johnny was his cousin's child, that was what the townspeople accepted as the truth. The gossipers he would ignore, like he always had. He heard them spreading their tales, like so many cow pies out in the pasture, for as many generations he had seen get born and die in that valley, much of it about himself and his sister. He minded his own business and would not let the talk get to him. However, one day he got a jolt of reality. The gossip he felt certain would be going around real soon, gave reason and forced Walter Henry to choose between letting Johnny grow up alongside his father and protecting him from his father.

It was morning and, with the boy at home feeling ill and being difficult to manage, Walter Henry was late coming down the hill to the blacksmith shop and livery stable. It was already open and, getting his work gloves on as he walked in, he heard Jim quietly talking with someone behind the barn at the back doorway. He could distinctly hear a woman's voice. Hesitating to step further into the barn, he turned about on his heels and walked back to his truck in time to see Forty Sumner's wife walking behind the buildings past the alleyway, between the blacksmith shop and the old Pine Way store. The post office and newspaper office were open, but it appeared that only Walter Henry saw what happened, though he was not sure what.

Pacing in front of the barn, he became furious, fed up with that "crazy as a coot young man," an opinion he dared breathe only to himself. He knew better than to deny what was going on between those two. He had heard plenty, back when Jim's father was still alive, lecturing his son about, "carryin' on with a girl like that," before the arguing would commence. Jim would yell at his father to stop telling him what to do. Walter Henry forgot all about that and here it was going on like it always had.

"What is it with those two, anyhow?" he asked himself.

Right when he contained his anger, and he rarely got mad, he pulled off his gloves one fingertip at a time. Raising his hand, he slammed them onto the ground, knowing at a glance that

Tucker Stewart was looking out the top window of the newspaper office. No matter. Walter Henry had seen plenty of "that Stewart clan" arguing amongst themselves to be at all worried. It always came down to this, he surmised, that if Edenville was a town too small for secrets, Pine Way was a town too small even for privacy.

He picked up his gloves and set about his day. Jim opened the stalls to the corral, so the horses could go outside. Next, he got them some clean water. Walter Henry observed him from across the barn. Jim was someone he had grown to love like his very own grandson, someone of whom he was proud. He was aware that Jim harbored great rage and inner pain, and felt aggrieved for the young man, because of it. He wanted Jim and his son to be together, to have what Walter Henry, himself, had lost. While he got the fire going in the forge, he felt constrained by the promise he and his sister had made to one another, not to tell Jim that Johnny was his child. It was worse than a secret. It was wrong, he believed, like it went against nature.

"Jim needs to know," he argued with that promise that was made.

The coals glowed brighter in the forge as he drew down the handle to the bellows. He looked across the barn into the livery stable and espied Jim setting the pitchfork aside to reach down into a keg, pull out a bottle, and take a swig from it. Turning away from what he had witnessed, the old blacksmith reached a decision.

Given all of Jim's problems, not only the boy's mother, but his father, were unfit to be proper parents. Walter Henry decided to adopt Johnny. He chose not to ask Jim or to tell him, which was regrettable. Although he knew he would have to say something, "when" never presented itself until, what felt like the right decision, turned into one of the worst mistakes he would make in his entire life. His other mistake was made years before, but he had yet to discover that one.

CHAPTER NINETEEN

Walter Henry convinced himself that he and his sister had done the right thing by adopting Johnny. Nevertheless, the entire process left him feeling saddened and sick to his stomach. Even though they were related, Johnny was put on record as an abandoned child. It brought tears to Walter Henry's eyes, making him love the boy all the more. The child became like a precious gift.

He placed the adoption papers in a metal box, under lock and key. Having a birth certificate, made it possible to enroll Johnny in school, a couple of years late, but it was all right. Though the boy was older than his classmates, it was not unusual for their rural school to have older teenagers and adults in elementary school, learning to read and write.

It worried the old man to see the decline in Jim's health and well-being. The times when he saw the young man he once knew, grew scarce. Drinking the hard stuff and "that Sumner woman," he said, was the beginning of the end. They fueled Jim's mounting temper outbursts and rages. He was thankful that, at least, Jim never got mad when Johnny was at the barn.

Walter Henry took his responsibility as a father very much to heart. School, friends, and chores kept the boy busy and they kept him safe, which was most important, not only to Walter Henry and Sister Ruth, but to Jim. Whenever they went to the barn, he had Johnny wait in the truck while he made sure all was well before he let the boy enter. Sometimes, "that Sumner woman" was already there, so Walter Henry had to take the boy home. Consequently, the boy and his real father were more and more apart from one another.

Despite efforts to control the situation, the boy loved Jim and would oftentimes sneak away from the house, from school, or from church, simply to be with the man he admired most. One time, he left Walter Henry's side at the community church and went across the street to the Catholic church to stand beside Jim during Mass. Jim placed a hand on the boy's shoulder, sharing the Sunday missalette with him. Johnny looked up at Jim with a big smile as though to say, "Thank you, Dad."

Johnny needed a real father, often pretending it was Jim, who really was his father. The man taught Johnny everything he knew about caring for horses, how to ride a horse, about being a farrier, even being a good man, like Jim's father had done.

Jim privately wished to honor his dad and pass on the business to his own son, Johnny. He hoped to make up for all the things he had said to his father out of anger. Though he continued to believe his dream to go to college had been dashed by his father's death, he lived his true dream with Johnny at his side.

"I'm proud of you," he would praise the boy as love filled his heart. "You take care of the horses real well." Or, "Look at that, Walt," he said, when he began teaching his son how to ride a horse. "He's a natural!" Once, he even said, "Good job, Son!"

He failed to catch it. It came out naturally, feeding the boy's desire to be Jim's son. Jim was Johnny's hero.

Unfortunately, the hour had arrived when it was too late for Walter Henry to tell Jim he had adopted Johnny. Johnny was in a fight at school and ran off to the livery stable. He went directly to Jim, scraped up, crying, and dirty. Jim caught him in his arms and lifted the boy up off the ground to hold him. Johnny shared, between sobs, what had happened. Before Jim knew what his partner had done, he was down at the school, letting them know what for, when the principal interrupted him.

"Excuse me. You're not the boy's father." the principal said. "Where's Mr. Henry?"

Jim almost shouted, "I'm the boy's father!" Although, stunned, he held himself back. He waited with Johnny until Walter Henry showed up, discovering that his business partner was his son's legal parent. It hit Jim like a punch in the gut.

When Walter Henry opened the door and saw Jim in the school's office, he knew he had done the wrong thing. He had not only stopped being a father figure for Jim, but he had stolen from Jim the right to be Johnny's father.

It made no difference to Johnny. In the boy's heart where words and official papers could not go, he would always love Jim as a son loves his dad.

When Jim left the office, on his way back to his truck, Katie came out of the school library. They saw one another. Her hair was long and dyed completely blond. She had it styled in something of a bouffant and was wearing a plain brown, wool skirt and matching jacket, a gold brooch on her lapel, nylon stockings, and plain, black, high-heeled shoes. She needed glasses, so she wore the fashionable cat eyes style, brown, complete with rhinestones. She almost started when she saw Jim, knowing full well who he was. He appeared to be in a hurry. In the mere seconds of their encounter, she had no time to act, only to notice him. Jim, however, failed to recognize her.

A brief feeling came over him when they made eye contact. Seated behind the wheel in his truck, he not only missed Katie, but he missed who he was when they were together. This awareness set him off and, in his bitterness, he spiraled downward into self-destruction.

He drove home in disgust and immediately called Sylvia. She came to the back door of the barn as he had instructed her to do. Once they were together inside, he locked the front door and locked the back door. He began, for the first time since before he married to do what he wanted to do, but had not the courage, as he saw it. He made Sylvia his and his alone, both vowing to be each other's one and only from then on. After several years of being absolutely faithful to his wife, Jim took the plunge off the deep end of his embattled soul. No one, not Katie, nor Johnny, nor any of his family would be able to bring him back.

He and Walter Henry spoke very little to one another for a long time. It was painfully grim around the blacksmith shop and livery stable. Jim never took it out on Johnny or Walter Henry, never got mad at them, but he took it out on himself and he took it to his grave. He loved the boy, not like a son, but as his son, which was apparent to all who saw them together, including the school's principal that one fateful day. Jim only saw his cowardice that prevented him from fighting for his son and making the changes needed, however difficult, to take on the responsibility of being the boy's father.

Jim eventually learned that Johnny discovered the truth. A few years later, while setting the pitchfork aside to reach into the nail keg and pull out the hidden bottle of booze, Jim heard Johnny call out to him.

"Dad!"

Johnny startled Jim, catching him off guard. He hurried to meet the boy with open arms.

Johnny was crying, saying, "I know you're my dad! Why can't I be with you?!"

Jim loved the boy and would not deny it, holding him like they had not seen one another in ten years. He grew disheartened, though, for he had cut his arm again earlier that day.

Beth had come home for lunch, so she could drink, and he was in the kitchen, having found something sharp. She had combed the house for anything he might try to use, and had asked a nurse to help her. The nurse appeared horrified by the state of the house, so Beth explained to her, "Between Jim's problems and work, it just got away from me," which was only half true, for her own problems were the other half.

Jim had managed to find something, or broke something. Beth had run into the kitchen, too late. He was on the floor, doing his rocking, holding the bloody cut and crying out loud, "I wish I could die! I just wanna die!"

After bandaging his cut, Beth telephoned the infirmary. She told the nurse it was time to call in for help, adding that she was no longer able to manage Jim. When the doctor showed up at the house, Jim was gone, having fled to the livery stable, with Johnny crying out, "I know you're my dad! Why can't I be with you?!"

Jim knelt before the boy and said, "I love you, Son. I've always known, ever since your mother brought you to us. I vowed to protect you and to love you as my son, but I couldn't keep you. I couldn't raise you."

Regardless of whether Johnny could understand the source, Jim unbuttoned his shirt sleeves and rolled them up to show his son the scars upon scars, plus the recent cut, bandaged only a few hours before.

"You see, Johnny," he said, "I can't take care of you. I never could. Your mother neither. Both of us are too—I mean, we wouldn't have been good for you, living with us. We couldn't have taken care of you." With that, Jim turned away from the boy and sat down, drawing his knees in close.

Johnny knelt beside his father and said, "At least we get to be together here. At least now we can stop pretending with each other." He placed a hand on his father's knee and asked, "Can I call you 'Dad', or, should we keep things the way they are?"

"Best to keep things the way they are, Johnny. I don't want to hurt Walt. He's done such a fine job raising you. I'm glad he did. He took care of you. He's been the father I couldn't be. Walt's a good man."

Johnny pulled from his shirt pocket a medal from Jim's high school graduation and a small scrapbook he had found that contained pictures of Jim's high school football career. He offered them to Jim, but all Jim said was, "You keep them, Son. You're my hero, now."

Johnny stood up and said, "See ya tomorrow, Da—" He looked down and said, "Jim," and left the barn.

Lowering his head, Jim buried his despair in his arms, confronted once more with the loss, the reality, and it being too much for such a man to overcome on his own. Looking toward the open door, toward the sunlight beyond the shadow cast by the once-imposing structure, Jim recalled the story of his great-grandfather, Josiah Hart. Death was near, he knew, inevitable and close. Pondering that place once called The Way, however, he knew he was not alone. Sensing someone standing beside him, perhaps a spirit, calmed him, allowing him to see what he needed to do. He saddled one of the horses and rode a trail no one else used, so he could think, and plan, without distraction.

CHAPTER TWENTY

The one-hundredth anniversary of the settling of Pine Valley began with one man's innocent announcement at the Parent-Teacher Advisory Group meeting one evening. Thanks to him, the historical date was mentioned amidst dropping jaws, blank stares, and a momentary lull in the meeting.

The chairman and president of P-TAG pounded his gavel and said, "The chair recognizes Harvey Cadwallader."

Harvey said, "As you all know, I am the Edenville Post Office postmaster," to which one man raised his voice and said, "we know who you are, Harvey!"

The timid man strived to regain his composure, much to the "good gawd's" and harrumphing of those present. They believed the meeting had gone on long enough. They wanted to get home to some tv show or movie over which they had been closely watching the clock.

Harvey began again after clearing his perpetually congested lungs. "As you all know," he said, "I am the Edenville Post Office postmaster, as well as a direct descendant of the very first postmaster in our valley." Again clearing his lungs with a cough, he drew a handkerchief from his pocket to expectorate into, then continued. "As such," he went on, "I have it on good authority that Pine Valley was settled one hundred years ago by autumn of next year. I propose we plan a celebration of sorts to commemorate this auspicious event."

Once the doe-eyed shock had passed, a rumble of discussion ensued. Even the chairman wanted to get home to his favorite tv show, so the proposal was voted on and quickly passed. A committee was formed out of those who lingered to partake of cookies, tea, coffee, or punch and, of course, clean up afterward. These dedicated citizens wholeheartedly agreed that, "Yes, there needs to be a celebration!"

Over the following days, various themes were shared, summarily discussed, and one chosen, that of an essay contest on the subject, "The Settlement of Pine Valley." Various categories were determined, based on age, whether professional or amateur. The winners would have their essay printed in *The Edenville Weekly* which, for this special issue alone, would be printed under its historical name of *The Pine Way Weekly Journal*. Excitement ran high in the newspaper office over what could be printed in the special edition. They agreed it needed to honor the historical significance of the times, possibly include some old advertisements and news items. One journalist commented that, perhaps, they could re-create the old-style newspaper in its entirety.

Ordinary citizens, such as Candelaria Hart, were inspired. She imagined what she would write about, "if I were a writer," she whispered one night before going to sleep. Her wish to become a writer coalesced in her dreams and in her visions. She imagined the life of her two grandfathers, Berto Mendoza and Joaquin Muscio, whom she knew, because it was always told to her, were the very first settlers of Pine Valley. Stories told by her mother and father, her Uncle Herman, her grandparents, and even Uncle Dexter Shows-His-Guns, filled her imagination. She thought of them as she dozed off to sleep each night, as she soaked in a tub of hot water, as she picked apples in the orchards, and as she walked to and from her mother's house. Even as she watched the clothes tumbling in the dryer at the laundromat, she dreamed. It was a beautiful story she would one day write. It would begin with her Papa Berto, who witnessed the first wagon trains arrive in Pine Valley.

•   •   •

In 1865, Berto Mendoza sat on the bank of the creek that flowed alongside the mountain's edge. He was working his small mining claim. The leaves of trees that bordered the creek shone brightly, like glistening, gold coins. Clattering and clapping in the wind, some were cast adrift into the clear blue of the sky. In a sudden, furious rush, the wind strengthened and blew like chargers 'fore the storm. A small flock of birds clung with tiny, stick-legged grips ahold of tree stems, swaying and bouncing about with the blustery flow of chill air. Any sound they made was lost to the roaring wind that thrashed the pine and the fir branches, some cracking and snapping loose to fall far down along the mountainside. One branch landed near Berto's feet. He leapt from his seat in surprise.

It was then that he saw, descending the canyon along a rocky path, several heavy wagons inching along, creaking in their heaving bulk, bumping and knocking side to side. Every roll of their great, wooden wheels threatened to snap and break them from their axles.

Long before their arrival, the furniture they held was cast off and abandoned along the wayside. Favorite pictures were removed from frames too heavy or too large, tossed away as so much junk. Soup tureens, tea sets, a trunk of fine dresses, a cabinet of books, were also left behind. However, among the absolute necessities being carried to the end of the trail, a weaving loom and a spinning wheel appeared questionable, but they could not be parted with, nor could a fiddle, a zither, and an exceptionally large, family bible.

The wagons carried families who were driven from their homes, only to be further ravaged by losses incurred along the trail. Guerrilla warfare in the heated confrontations along the borders had forced them to flee. Civil war and the greater trauma of slavery was not their fight in life, but they were nevertheless affected by it, drawn into the fray as though by a vacuum. If slavery, as some argued, was not the cause of the fight, it was what intensified the struggle and, thus, became like the eye of the needle through which all had to pass. When they and their neighbors took their stand against slavery, they were subsequently burned from their homes, driven off, thieved against. Some were killed. Their hope for a new land over the horizon's brim and the mountains upon mountains beyond, filled them and carried them westward each day, onward day after day and, ultimately, brought them home. Whereas the West called to thousands upon thousands, Pine Valley called only to a few. It was these few who arrived with a dream of peace for all.

One of the pioneers was Jebediah Walker. His wife died giving birth on the trail, their third child, who also died. He had two small children, Joseph and Jiminy, who yet needed care. Estefana Garcia, who had lost her parents in the guerrilla raid the year before, took it upon herself to help Jebediah, since she already rode with their wagon. She was terrified of fire since her parents were killed amidst flames. The pioneers were sure to place the girl under cover lest they all have none to warm themselves, or to cook by, or ward off the beasts that trailed them in the day and closed in on them in the night.

The lead wagon was driven by Cedric Cadwallader. His eldest son had become old enough to help out with the men, calming frantic teams, unloading wagons for treacherous sections of the trail, stream crossings, and broken axles. Cedric's once huge family of ten children was tragically reduced to five by the fever that struck, before they had even embarked upon their trek. Cedric's wagon was followed by that of Thomas McGrew, with his wife and young son, Ulysses. Next, came the Walker's with the orphan, Estefana Garcia, holding the youngest in her arms.

No matter where they positioned themselves in the snake-like course of the wagon train, Bartholomew Jones insisted on being in the rear.

"To be sure no one gets forgotten or left behind," he said.

Bart had lost his wife, her lone burial left behind in the desert-like sagebrush country through which they had passed.

"She will sleep uneasy, bein' so alone," he said. "Only that mournful coyote will sing to her now, and that cryin' wind."

To the gray-clouded emptiness above, he cast his prayers and, turning his horse about, rode on to catch the others. He left his wagon behind, an axle broken, which is how his wife had died, having been killed when the wagon toppled. From that time forward, he always scouted ahead or swept the rear for stragglers.

In Pine Valley, the wagon trail and the creek below made a gradual turn toward the south at the base of the mountainside.

Here, the light of the sun shone like bright rays striking through the shadowy forest. Enlivened, the coming families began cheering, talking, and laughing.

"I think we're almost there!"

"Hold your team!"

"What d'ya think, Cedric?"

Cedric, the Welshman, shouted, "It will be the land of my dreams!" Thrilled by the sight, he sang, "Give me fair and bonny land to rest my weary head. 'Tis only what I pray for thee, my love, my darling, Enid."

Berto, yet standing in awe of the coming spectacle, was startled by a dog splashing into the water, barking at him.

"Que?!" Berto jumped away. He shouted at the dog. "No, perro! No!" he said.

He ran up the trail to his ramshackle, makeshift miner's cabin to survey the coming parade of Pine Valley history in the making. Calling out to his mining partner, he said, "Quino! Ven! Ven aqui!"

His friend, Joaquin, set aside his coffee to hurry over to Berto.

"Mira!" Berto said in his worry while pointing to the large wagons coming. Their once-white canvas covers were a bleak and dusty gray. The bearing of their stalwart purpose was written in burned holes, gouged wood, lumbering teams of oxen, mules, and drooling, limping horses, faithful to their end in Pine Valley.

Berto's future flashed before his eyes. It was bad enough when wagon trains arrived the previous year, as far as a reclusive soul such as himself was concerned. Even though only two families had stayed, seeing more arrive was, nonetheless, disheartening.

On the spot, Berto said, "There goes the last of our quiet days, eh, Quino? It will be a fight from here on. For, now, this is no longer merely a camp, mi amigo. It has become a town, and a town is no place for me."

CHAPTER TWENTY-ONE

Years before his arrival in Pine Valley, Berto Mendoza sat astride a gray horse looking northward across the Mexican desert. With only a broad sombrero to protect him from the harsh sunlight, he set out in search of mountains. Stories told of vast ranches further north, where cattle grazed in a rangeland of grasses that grew taller than a man. It was where a man could prosper and make a life for himself on his own terms. However, the stories he had heard about this promise land, turned out to be only partly true. Cattle once numbering in the hundreds of thousands were severely impacted by drought. Rangeland once supporting tall and lush vegetation was decimated by the enormous herds of cattle and sheep, leaving behind a ruined landscape. Every river, stream, and watering hole was putrified by their waste. Nothing was untouched by the insatiable beasts Berto grew to dislike. Being a shy fellow, he drew further inward-dwelling, contemplating a fitting likeness between the gluttonous herds and their ever-greedy landowners.

His heart no longer in it, Berto made up his mind to leave the rugged life of a cowpuncher. He said goodbye to his one friend and fellow countryman, Joaquin Muscio, and departed. The distant view of snow-covered mountains rising in the east, like the very ascent into heaven, called to him, he confided in Joaquin. Several days after he rode away, he stumbled upon a quiet, forested valley with a creek that flowed alongside its mountainous edge. His meager skills in mining revealed that it contained gold. Sending word to his friend, it was not long before Joaquin joined him and, together, they led an uneventful life overlooking Pine Valley.

The original people who once lived there, but who had been driven out years before, had returned. They peacefully resided in a hidden meadow immediately to the south of the valley floor. One day, the tribe's patriarch paid the miners a visit. Soon afterward, Berto visited the tribe's encampment. His eyes beheld a young woman, Lucy Shoseegan, the same, pretty girl Joaquin had recently met, and about whom he avoided telling his friend. While Joaquin was away on a hunting trip, Berto paid Lucy special attention. He was neither cowboy nor hunter and carried no guns. It turned out, he was a lover. He spoke tenderly to Lucy and she smiled. Though not understanding the Spanish words Berto spoke, she understood the feeling with which he said them, gently holding her hand and wooing her with his heart-song. Joaquin returned, discovering what had taken place while his back was turned. His friend had stolen the pretty native girl from him.

Upset and brooding, Joaquin grew annoyed with Berto. So, he left again and went back to work as a ranch hand, which he did fairly well. In the meantime, Berto made Lucy his wife, nicknaming her "Choocha." They were first married in the tradition of her people, but were later married in the tradition of his own when a Catholic priest traveled through the area. By then, the mission padre was not only baptizing Lucy, but her and Berto's three children, Jesse, Hermenegildo, and Manuel. The settlers in the valley soon nicknamed the middle son, "Herman," and the youngest son, "Manny."

When Berto's sons were old enough, they joined him in his small mining venture. He traveled to the state capital to sell his gold, keeping the amounts small, so as not to attract any notice. The years passed and Berto's sons grew up as their mining venture wound down. Berto and Lucy then lived off the land as her people had done all their lives and as Berto had learned back in Mexico. He made himself a gathering pouch like the one his wife carried. Together, they foraged afield. Lucy sang to the plants as she expertly tended them. Berto followed suit in his homespun woolen clothes so worn that they had patches upon patches. They both wore shoes made from woven strands of peeled bark. Berto's sombrero long lost, he also made himself a type of hat from the bark. He let his hair grow long, like Lucy's, even braided it. Adopting his wife's reclusiveness, he let his sons go to town while he wrote poetry and dreamed of a better world.

Seated on a large stone he used as his lookout over the valley and the stream below, he drank his coffee and dwelled on the ills of the world beyond their little bit of heaven. He saw the imbalance of power, the social elitism, the rich businessmen, the land barons, and the officials their money elected into office to serve them and their needs. People, like himself, who only wanted to live peaceably, to love their fellow citizens, for there to be harmony, to help those in need, to care for those too old or sick to care for themselves...well, they saw opportunities, too. Although, these were within a social structure and an economic system of which they were not a part, nor in which they felt welcome. To Berto, who saw two worlds, one for the rich and one for the poor who worked for and made the rich richer, people like him were not welcome simply because they cared. They had heart. They wanted to share what little they had with others. For anyone to be so wealthy, so far removed from the lives of ordinary people, and for it to serve only themselves, he believed to be unnatural, a form of insanity bred by greed and endless acquisitiveness.

By the campfire outside their mining shack home, Berto discussed these issues with his sons. His dear Choocha cooked over the fire or tended it, chiming in with her own observations.

"You talk of what I know, Berto," she said. "I do all the work and you give all the orders."

At this, Berto laughed and pulled her down to sit beside him as he hugged and kissed her. Their sons smiled sheepishly and laughed with them.

Herman took his father's words to heart and longed to take advantage of the opportunities of which his father spoke. He wanted to travel, to attend college, and to become a journalist, so he could write about these things. He pictured himself speaking for those too beaten down and oppressed to speak for themselves, namely, the Mexican people under a rule his father vividly described.

Bidding a teary farewell to his parents and his two brothers, he mounted his horse and set off for his father's homeland. With a letter for his father's family and prayers for a safe journey, Herman headed south for Mexico. Several years passed, but he eventually returned and the family was together again. He sported a mustache and his thick curly hair that always grew upward in a bushy mass, was neatly trimmed. He brought stories to share around the campfire, accounts of political upheaval and oppression of the Mexican peasantry that was so egregious, that many were calling for change, for "revolución."

Herman had completed college and became a journalist, along with many of the intellectuals of his age. In Mexico, he and his fellow activists printed their own newspapers and disseminated subversive literature. They posted political handbills on fenceposts and buildings, anywhere their message could be seen. Meeting in secret, they held discussions in small huts, dark corners of a cantina, and caves along the cliffs of the river winding its way far below. They strived to reach even the poorest of the poor whose communal grazing lands were taken from them, those who were struck down if they dared to fight. These desperate measures called for the people to rise up and take a stand.

Berto listened to his son and, without hesitating, encouraged him to go to work for the newspaperman in town, Harry Stewart. He told Herman that Harry long complained that none of his sons wanted to stay and work on the paper. Harry yet had hopes for his youngest son, Tucker Howard Stewart, but it was still too soon to tell. The boy had barely begun school. The only thing a six-year-old could do at a newspaper office was a somewhat passable job of sweeping the floors and emptying the trash bins. Berto made sure to stress with his son, not to mention he returned when he had, because he was thrown out of Mexico.

Herman was driven away, escorted at rifle point by a government detachment of soldiers. They charged him with planning an insurrection and inciting a mob which led to rioting in the streets of a village in northern Mexico. Unfortunately, he was singled out by his own comrades as the sole perpetrator of actions culminating in the only building not made of adobe or stone, but of lumber, to be burned to the ground. It was the home of an American missionary and his wife.

Herman was welcomed aboard by Harry Stewart, whose fat fingers held his even fatter cigar. He plugged the corner of his grinning mouth with it, so he could shake Herman's hand vigorously and reassure the young college graduate.

"You won't regret it, young man," he said. "This will be the best damned frontier newspaper by the turn of the century. By golly! Let's get to work, shall we?"

Harrison Stewart, the lone newspaperman for years, could finally put together a substantial newspaper. With Herman's help and eager willingness to travel and obtain detailed news on stories near and far, big news stories were included, all of which Harry was proud. He finally had something he could mail back home to show his own family he had made good of their faith in him.

One evening, Herman stood at the edge of his family's clearing, looking out across Pine Valley. His brother, Manny, approached him and asked what it was like in Mexico, specifically the women.

"Were they beautiful, Herman?" he asked.

Manny was the youngest, eager to go out into the world and get married, thinking only of practical matters. Though still young, he imagined life as a cowboy and the women he might encounter, perhaps wanting only to comfort a lonely young man.

"Yes," Herman replied with reservation, "there were some women who were very beautiful."

Manny grew concerned. His brother left it at that. He wanted to hear details, stories of his brother's passionate adventures.

"Herman, tell me, how beautiful?" he asked. "Did you go to bed with any of them?"

Manny's eyes widened and a grin grew on his face. He eagerly awaited the full, steamy and exciting story, but none followed. His brother merely stood, watching the sun go down. Manny thought his brother was avoiding him.

"What's wrong, Herman?" he asked.

Herman appeared as though he gazed upon the stars, but he was seeing what had taken place far away in Mexico. On a quiet night in a humble village, he said his goodbyes to someone he left behind. The sadness of this loss rose to the surface.

One by one, in the valley below where they stood, lanterns were lit in homes. Voices murmured like water running over stones, bubbling softly along. The last light departed into the golden evening as a multitude of stars awakened like beacons from another world glimmering far above. Herman's eyes reflected what light there was as he freely wept. He could find no words to describe the horrible atrocities he had witnessed, gory scenes that haunted him, the lowness that the rich would stoop to secure their power.

"Herman, tell me." Manny drew closer to him. "What's wrong? Why do you not answer me?"

Herman looked at his brother with such sorrow in his eyes, yet also with a degree of surrender, not knowing what to say to Manny or how he might take it. Yet, he could only speak the truth.

"Yes, Manny," he said, "there were many beautiful women, but there were also many beautiful men. Do you understand what I am saying?"

Manny's eyes grew wider, this time in horror, as though his brother said he had murdered and done despicable things to the bodies. He understood, but was disgusted.

He asked his brother, "What are you saying, Herman? That you-you went to bed with-with men?"

Herman regretted telling his secret to Manny, who, without delay, left his side, said goodbye to their parents, and saddled his horse. Before departing, he told his brother, "You can tell Papá, I like the idea of becoming a land baron." He mounted his horse and said, "Unbridled greed and 'subjugation of the meek and teeming masses' sounds pretty good to me," and laughed as he rode off. Aside from Christmas for a couple of years, the family did not see Manuel again until he had married and had, himself, a son.

Herman told no one of his secret ever again and kept that part of his life to himself. He especially kept secret his private trips to the state capital. He had learned of places where he could safely meet other men like himself and thereby socialize in genteel establishments.

Years later, when Herman was a middle-aged man, he befriended his boss's grandson, Dewey Stewart. Dewey had arrived home from the Second World War. Herman learned from him that it was not only the atrocities Dewey had witnessed that haunted his soul. It was the fact that he preferred the company of other men. He confided in Herman one day when they were left alone in the office to close up shop.

Dewey was upset when he said, "I didn't want to be this way." He was tortured by guilt and shame. He was angry with the God of his family's church who condemned people like himself. "This is how God made me," he said. "I didn't choose it! No one would!"

On the second floor of the newspaper building, Herman sat at his desk, his serious expression belying the complete and utter compassion he felt while listening to his young co-worker speak the truth.

"Why?!" Dewey pleaded with Herman.

The young man suffered in silence and in secrecy, himself making the mistake of telling the wrong person, the priest, Father Jovial.

"Such activities are the work of the Devil, young man!" warned the priest. "You must forsake these feelings and the life it leads to. Search for salvation and forgiveness."

Father Jovial could forgive many things, but not this, for his own brother led such a life and was brutally beaten for it. He feared Dewey might end up like his brother.

Dewey's last words to Father Jovial, his confession, ended with, "I'm not strong enough, Father. It's like there's a great big hole that's come for me and I can't escape it!"

Herman knew Dewey was not motivated to suicide so much by the grisly memory of war, which Herman, himself, knew from experience during his time in pre-revolutionary Mexico. He knew Dewey was brought to suicide by sheer anguish and rage at a world that would not love him as he was, a man the way God had made him. This epiphany struck Herman with its significance: The way God made him, and all men like himself, even women. But, he wondered, why was it so?

•   •   •

It was no secret that Berto was unhappy with a town growing below his humble shack. So, after a time, he and Lucy packed their horses with what few belongings they owned and set off on the long trail, accompanied by their son, Herman. They traveled deeper into the mountains to a small village known as Laketon, where Lucy's family had retreated. Continuing to lead a simple life, Berto did as always, gathering the children around the campfire built by his patient and devoted wife while he told stories of Old Mexico, the land of his youth.

CHAPTER TWENTY-TWO

The schools in Edenville, both elementary and high school, planned their own essay contests to commemorate the settling of Pine Valley. After announcing it among their students, Johnny Henry planned to write about the stories his adoptive father, Walter Henry, had told him. These stories were among those handed down and, although there was joy in the telling, the remembering brought sadness as well. After all, Walter Henry was becoming an old man and found that little remained of those days he fondly shared with his son, Johnny.

The story began when Henry Henry and his young bride drove their wagon up the last weary climb to Pine Valley. With his father's crude, hand-drawn map to guide them to the spot, their arrival was filled with an innocent hopefulness. It soon turned into anxious disappointment once they discovered they were not alone.

They soon met other settlers who shared their plans to build Pine Way, their cherished dream of a town far from the strife and struggle that lay eastward. He learned that three of them, Thomas McGrew, Jebediah Walker, and Bartholomew Jones had all applied for and were granted homesteads. They were settlers, they proudly told Henry Henry, and they meant to stay. From talking with them, the Henry's learned of the two Mexican men living there who were prospectors. He was told they spoke very little English, but were friendly, associating primarily with the native residents, adding that one had even married a native. Unperturbed by the settlers' subtle consternation regarding the other people with whom they shared the valley, the Henry's went to meet the prospectors and native families, too. They were determined to establish themselves amongst all who lived in Pine Valley.

Proving themselves to be of sound character, the Henry's soon got along with everyone and set about establishing their own encampment and home place. It was at the very entrance to Pine Valley from the western advance on the trail and at the point of exiting the valley, if one were traveling from the east. They brought with them a wealth of supplies, such as seeds, roots, and tubers, sacks of flour, grains, and beans, all of which needed protection from the weather and from rodents and other animals. They pitched their tent and, thus, took their first steps at providing for themselves. Fortunately, for Henrietta, who was not accustomed to living off the land, there were many others who could show her how. She had become a frontier woman and needed to learn how to derive a living from whatever lay at hand.

They often shared campfires and meals, but Henry Henry had plans of his own that did not agree with the settlers' ideas. He wanted to build a way station, a blacksmith shop, and a livery stable. He rode into the capital with his new friend, Hector Shoseegan, to apply for his own homestead. He advised Hector to do the same, to protect what little remained of their homeland. Henry Henry received a one-hundred-and-sixty-acre piece of land. Hector was merely informed about a rancheria created for tribes in their mountain region.

Surveyors walked the land, outlining the boundaries of each homestead. The land set aside for Hector and his people was predominately unusable for farming or grazing, land that none of the settlers wanted. Located on the mountain slopes at the eastern edge of the valley, it included the hillside where Berto and Joaquin's shack was built. Hector assured them they were welcome to stay, seeing as how Berto had married Hector's daughter. It was also discovered that the main village site of Hector's tribe also lay within the rancheria boundaries. On this portion, Berto's son, Jesse, would one day build his house for his new wife, Ev, and her mother, Estefana.

The settlers attempted to teach the others English, such as their own command of the language could afford. Using these basic rudiments, Henry Henry was able to convey to Hector his plans. Hector listened as they traveled homeward from their trip to the capital, followed by a freight wagon loaded with supplies, tools, and other necessities. They became friends, despite the uneasiness Henry Henry felt in the presence of someone who carried two pistols in a double holster slung around his hips. Hector and his son, Dexter, were both armed men, something with which their new friend was uncomfortable. He shared with Hector his dream of creating a town, a place where everyone lived in peace with one another. Hector liked that, to welcome others in need of fellowship, a community even he and his family wanted.

Hector and the two prospectors found it useful to learn English. It was a valuable tool in their new life. It protected Hector and his family, helping them to blend in with the growing community. For the two miners, it served them equally well.

Having lost his first love to his friend, Berto, Joaquin turned his eye to the orphan, Estefana Garcia, who lived with Hector's people. They called her Little Fawn. The young woman was proficient at both English and Spanish and had also learned the tribe's language, finding herself in the valuable position of interpreter. This greatly impressed Joaquin who paid her visits under the guise of learning English from her.

Pioneers continued to travel the route that came over the mountains from the east and passed through Pine Valley on their way to the great valley beyond. Many traveled in the opposite direction, dreamers on their way to the gold fields and settlers unhappy with the climate who were returning home. For these, and a variety of other reasons, the road was busy. Out of necessity, and very unceremoniously, Henry Henry pounded a makeshift sign into the ground across from his camp. From then on, travelers who passed through could see what the burgeoning town was named. It was not "Pine Way."

Despite its crude, makeshift accommodations, the Henry's acted in an official manner. When wagon trains, lone horsemen, and others passed through, they were asked to either line up, one behind the other, as with wagons, or hitch their horses out front of the Henry's canvas tent cabin, dubbed, "Pine Valley Way Station." A corral made of small trees that were chopped down, was erected beside a rough bark plank shack. Only three-sided, the shack utilized the trail's cut-bank as its rear wall. Its roof was merely a thatch of sorts, willow poles cut and arranged across the top as rafters, with pine boughs spread across them to make a roof.

The Henry's strived to accomplish more their first year. But, their time was taken up with the sheer survival of day to day living. Additionally, Henrietta was expecting their first child.

Humbled by adversity, they were overcome with gratitude when the settlers offered to help build a permanent way station and barn. Agreeing to the settlers' terms, the Henry's dedicated a small portion of their homestead for a proper town.

Like the Henry's, the settlers had made some progress building their homes and outbuildings, corrals, and chicken coops, and they began planting fruit orchards. Even though the naming of the town had been conducted in a high-handed fashion, with some arguing it was "downright underhanded," they saw that Henry Henry's plans basically fit in with their own. So, they bided their time. With the men working together, they commenced construction on a fine and sturdy way station. Trees began to fall, and the sound of cracking, splintering branches were followed by resounding thuds heard across the valley. Progress, they all commented, had finally begun.

When completed, the way station would be a two-story building of milled lumber made from their own trees, though milled off-site, since they did not yet have their own sawmill. It would include the Henry's living quarters, kitchen, dining area, and parlor on the lower level. The top floor would be partitioned into four large rooms, later divided into eight smaller rooms, for guest lodging, and that was about all they were, bare rooms. The Henry's needed to acquire or build furniture, make rugs and practically everything. However, they could not make a cookstove. Henry Henry planned to go to the nearest large town to purchase one, thankful his wife would be looked after, in the event the baby should come while he was away. However, he could not leave until the building was completed. The finishing touch was a fine porch for sitting and greeting visitors. He knew what his first, personal wood projects would be, a cradle for the baby and a rocking chair for his wife, but how he would find the time for that, he had no idea. Once the way station was complete, he hurried off, thanking everyone for their help in making the place a real town. He knew some of them yet lived very primitively until their own homes were built.

On his way down the road, a very pregnant Henrietta shouted a last minute request.

"A bathtub, Henry!" she said, her hand placed alongside her mouth. "Don't forget a bathtub!"

"Yes, Henrietta," he said and waved his hand to signal that he had heard.

After he returned, work began on the barn, which would be the largest building in the valley for decades to come. The way station would one day follow the demise of the horse and buggy. The barn, on the other hand, was built to last. It had solid oak beams, laid upon heavy stones dug into the earth as the foundation. Pine and fir was used for the walls and, again, heavy oak beams were hoisted high above to brace the walls and support the roof. With a loft for hay and individual stalls, plus a large corral, the livery stable was fairly completed, as was the barn. No tree was thought too lowly for use. The barn would need all the wood they could cut, with even maple and black walnut finding a place in the finished structure. Felled trees of an exceptionally huge size were discovered at a distance from Pine Valley in groves of magnificent, living giants. The enormous amounts of lumber they could provide, turned out to be a fool's errand, for they had very little practical use other than for making fences, roofing shingles, or firewood.

The blacksmith's shop with forge and implements were something Henry Henry wanted to make on his own. He was a blacksmith by trade and, though he was handy with woodcarving, his skill as a blacksmith was well-known. A sturdy work bench was constructed out of oak and maple and he hauled brick for his forge from down in the valley, where he learned that bricks were being made. He began to fashion tools and implements, including the andirons for the way station's fireplace. They were unadorned except for the front supports that were tall and sturdy enough to hold large logs in place, to prevent them from rolling out onto the floor. At the top of each post, he fashioned the shapes of pine cones.

Henrietta was pleased and, despite the struggles of their first two years, she was happier than she could remember.

"It's beautiful, Henry," she said. "Guests will enjoy socializing before the fire with coffee and doughnuts."

The baby arrived during all the activity, their first child, Lulabelle. Henrietta's sister-in-law, Rebecca, came to help. She ended up staying, hoping to marry and raise a family there, herself.

The days never ended at the way station. Besides a crying infant all day and all night, there was always work to be done. Henrietta was exhausting herself, even with Rebecca's help, until Estefana Garcia came to work for her. Estefana had a baby of her own and took up residence in the way station with them, so there were two crying babies. The two toddlers ran after their mothers on busy work days, with Ev Garcia learning how to do work and Lulabelle learning how to avoid it. Ev wanted to do everything with her mother, to be by her side helping. Lulabelle provided the guests with odd forms of entertainment.

Ev stayed close to her mother's legs, rushing to help, even screaming if she could not do it without any help from her mother. When she screamed or screeched, her whole body would become rigid, her eyes stare, her hands ball up into fists, until she got her way. Each room had Ev's tiny-fisted signature on it, towels sometimes in a bunched-up wad instead of being neatly folded. The laundry basket ofttimes banged its way down the stairs, either bumping each step as Ev pulled it, or rolling down as she merely pushed it, dirty linens and towels spilling along the way. Her well-known shriek informed Henrietta that little Ev was helping again.

Lulabelle, on the other hand, preferred to run wild in the great outdoors and would daily have some critter or another to bring into the parlor. Once, it was an orphaned fox kit she snuck into bed with her at night. Like a proud and tender mother, she would show it off to guests, the baby fox carefully swaddled in a small blanket. Lulabelle's face was always smeared with some mixture of dirt and whatever she had eaten last. Her hands always looked begrimed, with her clothes and hair in shabby disarray. Any attempt to comb her hair or bathe her were met with loud and sometimes piercing yowls, "exactly like a coyote pup," remarked one guest.

Ev insisted on having a miniature version of her mother's housekeeper's apron and duster cap. She kept her clothes neat and tidy, with black stockings, and black hair ribbons to tie her wavy, curly hair in one or two pony tails. She was not always that prim and proper, for she had a streak of the scalawag in her as well. Berto Mendoza's sons discovered this when they were sent on errands into town. They caught Ev climbing trees with Lulabelle and cannonballing unsuspecting guests with pine or fir cones. When the Mendoza boys shouted to expose the offenders to the guests, Ev would stick out her tongue and hurry back into the way station, leaving Lulabelle to receive the scoldings. Ev mostly stayed indoors helping her mother. She also learned to sing beautifully while she worked. One guest complimented her talent, so Ev occasionally treated the guests to a song, perhaps adding a dance in accompaniment, which brought smiles, genteel laughter, and applause.

However, Lulabelle would not be outdone, and became determined to "de-prissify that Garcia girl." While Ev was singing a tune for guests, Lulabelle crept into the parlor where she was strictly forbidden, due to the following sort of behavior. She loved to horrify or, at the very least, startle the guests with her own unique brand of entertainment. Since she would not do anything she was told, she hid in a corner while young Ev was singing for the guests. They were settled before the fire, sipping coffee and nibbling on their doughnuts. One man, whose dessert plate was precariously perched upon his ample waistline, was dozing off in the softly lit room when a chipmunk appeared on the scene. Ev's eyes grew wide, appalled at Lulabelle's nerve, yet refused to let it ruin her performance. The minuscule chipmunk's piping squeak broke the pleasant evening reverie so suddenly, that the small plate was flung into the air while others spilled their coffee or choked on crumbs. Amidst the stir, Ev sang louder, giving her personalized rendition of The Star-Spangled Banner.

"Oh, pay, it's not free!"

Once, was all it took, before guests learned who was really in charge and to be wary of both girls, be it the scruffy ragamuffin or the impish darling. They knew Ev was a girl, but they wondered if the so-named, "Lulabelle," was actually a misnomered boy. The guests who caught on, had fun watching newly arrived guests holler and wiggle when a lizard was let loose down their shirt collars. They were tickled to see the most proper among them leap from their chairs when garter snakes were released to slither around their feet. One evening, a wounded woodpecker, broken wing flopping uselessly at its side, clung to draperies, cloth-backed chairs, even one woman's dress, during her hysterical, panic-driven flight around the room. One man broke out in a fit of the giggling guffaws, having been sipping from brandy-laced coffee. A field mouse was let loose one time, chasing after an insect, which Lulabelle pulled by a string across the floor from where she hid under a table.

Henrietta's husband stayed late in the barn every night. She learned to warn their guests beforehand of their "unusual evening activities and daytime disturbances." She begged for their patience, asking them to forgive the children, "bless their hearts," she said.

Life carried on for the families with their growing town always referred to as Pine Way, except in the presence of Henry Henry. Guests not forewarned would barely even breathe the name, Pine Way, before he would shake his frazzled, frizzy hair and declare loudly to anyone who could hear him, "The Way! This town is called The Way!"

Enough of these incidents occurred that he decided it was time to erect an official welcome sign. No town council, as yet, was organized, so Henry Henry declared himself a council of one, for all he cared. He carved a sign into the late hours of the night. One morning, very grumpily, he yanked out the temporary sign and dug a hole within which he planted the new sign. Filling in the hole with rocks and dirt, then packing it down until the sign was secure, he completed his task.

"Welcome to The Way," it read to open-mouthed amazement and Henrietta's embarrassment.

Henry Henry walked away, tools in hand, amidst the small crowd of onlookers that had assembled. He gave his head a poignant nod and said, "There! It's final!" They could yet hear him on his way back into the barn when he said, "And I don't want to hear another word about it!"

However, the matter did not end there, so more late nights were devoted to his very own mission statement. Hand-carved on a beautiful slab of maple, whose grain formed curlicues and swirls, what some would call, "birds eye," it expressed his love for the little town. He planned to mount the plaque on the outside wall of the way station, by the front door, so all guests and visitors could read, "The Story of The Way."

CHAPTER TWENTY-THREE

Many of the settlers complained, because their town was not officially named Pine Way. Yet, they kept silent as they prepared to build their store, post office, and newspaper office. Brick structures were agreed upon for these, with wooden window frames, doors, and porches. Wood flooring of a heavy, sturdy grade was an absolute necessity to withstand a beating it would surely receive in a frontier landscape. Wood for lumber was in abundance, but where would they find enough brick, or afford it, for that matter?

Henry Henry assured them that the brick factory in the valley would supply their needs and told them not to worry about the cost. So, they started planning for the trip. Wagons were stripped bare for hauling loads of brick. Teams were readied for the week-long journey to and from the brick making plant. Orders were in from wives, requesting additional items.

One evening, when campfires were lit and lanterns were carried to light their way, they gathered for a final talk.

"This'll be no easy feat," said Bartholomew Jones. Bart was a big man with a big heart and a gentle soul. He added, "You all know I lost my wagon, but I'll be damned if I let you do this on your own." Looking to each man gathered there, he said, "So, you can count me in."

Nodding his head, Cedric said, "Happy to have you, Bart. Happy to have you." To all the men, he said, "Bart's right. It's not gonna be easy. But, this trip's long overdue." Pausing for a moment, he then added, "So...if we're gonna have a post office, we'll need a town, I figure. And, I think we ought to register it...or, some such thing...so Pine Way can go on the map."

"Now, you wait just a minute there!" warned Henry Henry. Jabbing his finger toward the ground to make his point, he said, "This town is still called The Way last time I checked."

"All right, Henry," said Cedric, raising his hands to silence the man. "Calm down," he said. "Nobody's saying nothing about changing the town's name or anything like that." Stroking his immense mustache, he gave a nervous, but knowing glance to the other men. "Whatever it's called," he continued, "we still need to register it somehow and, um, while we're on the subject..I was thinkin'...I would be the most logical choice for postmaster, wouldn't you say? Seein' as how I was a telegraph operator before we came out West here."

No one argued with him, so Cedric breathed a sigh of relief, hooking his thumbs around his suspenders and grinning.

• • •

In the wagon train years before, Cedric Cadwallader led the way and Bartholomew Jones took up the rear. They did so again on this trip. The excitement was contagious, almost festive, yet nothing could dispel the fears of those who were left behind, mostly women and young children. To dispel their fears,

Henrietta invited those without homes to be sheltered temporarily in the way station for protection.

Hector and his son, Dexter, along with Berto Mendoza and Joaquin Muscio, watched over the valley and its vulnerable residents. They provided fresh meat and everything the wilds had to offer. The week-long trip became two. So, young boys left behind were then taught how to live off the land. A few of the women, hardened and toughened on the emigrant trail and their frontier life, took to foraging and fashioning necessary items for their diet and for their comfort.

Unfamiliar with the plants in their new home, they soon learned how to treat a fever, how to make a mattress, and which plants were used to flavor meat. Young boys thrilled at lessons on how to track animals and birds. Young wives, whose mothers back East may have seen to their training in needlepoint and knitting, maybe dying graying hair, were eager to stretch their knowledge to include dressing a kill, cleaning a fish, and making an earthen oven. They were eager to learn and quick to appreciate their teachers.

Despite his misgivings about the town daring to exist below his humble life on the mountainside above, Berto could not refrain from simply caring. It was he who brought this gift to their valley which, in his long life, he taught by example. He showed kindness toward all and spoke passionately about the down-trodden masses, the poor, the starving, and the weak. Having willing students, as two weeks absence of the menfolk became three, he gave lessons in compassion. Rambling on in Spanish, English, and the native's language, he showed where to find the best blackberries and raspberries, which mushrooms could be eaten and which to avoid, where to find wild onions and hazelnut trees.

"Always remember," his typical sermons began, "leave some for the animals and the birds. Don't take it all for yourselves. Never, never. We must share with them all that the Lord provides. Just like the poor. We must share with them equally, because we are all the same in the eyes of the Lord."

Once the other men returned and the supplies were unloaded and distributed, wives shared with their husbands what they had done in their absence. Each embellished on exciting tales of survival. Each confirmed to the other, regarding Berto's quaint assistance, so that he, alone, was elevated to sainthood, exalted and held in their views as, "their savior." This was irregardless of all the help Hector and his family had given, and Joaquin, though they were certainly acknowledged.

Soon, each of the settlers visited Berto's mining shack with small tokens of appreciation.

Berto exclaimed, "Why, they treat me as though I had performed miracles!"

Humbled by the settlers' kindness, Berto offered much of what he was given to Hector and Dexter. They declined his offer, saying Berto's wife was soon to be a mother. She would need these things. Berto insisted, so his friends finally agreed on a box of cartridges, for which Berto had no use, and a very fine pocket knife Dexter had admired. Everyone was satisfied, except Joaquin. He was feeling uncomfortably civilized and disappeared for a time.

"Like a tumbleweed," one of the settlers remarked. "Nothing can keep that man from rolling on, here, then there, whichever way the wind blows."

Sitting on his overlooking stone, Berto listened as work on the new town proceeded once again. Hammering and shouting, laughter and orders being given echoed in their industrious activity below. He even heard a sawmill running. It was established by a newcomer to their valley who, upon hearing the men talk about their new settlement, asked if he could join them in building a town. They welcomed him, not knowing what that entailed. Tagging along behind him and his sister, were his motherless, though grown children, a milk cow, two goats, plus a small cart carrying a dozen laying hens and a pair of rabbits. Bartholomew Jones was thankful, because he received extra-special attention from the sawyer's widowed sister. She and Bart were soon married. Years later, they had a daughter, Adelaide Jones, who would one day marry Tucker Howard Stewart.

The day arrived when Henry Henry discovered that his funds had dwindled so low, he was broke. His wife's dowry and generous wedding gifts of cash were all gone. Yet, business was booming. Word spread of their new town and travelers came to or from across the mountains, hearing news of the lovely way station.

Cedric Cadwallader was the town's first postmaster. When citizens began to mail their first letters, they stepped into the brand new post office, greeted by Cedric and his very large and bushy mustache. He stood behind the counter wearing his new visor and wire-rimmed glasses, addressing everyone with a heavy Welsh accent.

"Welcome to Pine Way Post Office!" he said. Unless, of course, it was one of the Henry's. Then, Cedric would greet them by saying, "Welcome! Welcome! What can I do for you?"

Whatever he said, he always smiled and beamed with pride. He kept his apron spotless, carried out his work with an attitude of professionalism, and ran the office efficiently. He served the town well, until his son, Bill, was hired, becoming their second postmaster. Bill's nephew, Geoffrey Cadwallader, later ran the post office. By the 1960s, when Pine Way was becoming a forgotten place, Geoffrey's son, Harvey, became postmaster. It was he who informed the Edenville Elementary School Parent-Teacher Advisory Group meeting about the one-hundredth anniversary.

Thomas McGrew and his son, Ulysses, ran the Pine Way General Store. Ulysses' eldest son, Sam, took over until the store went out of business, unable to keep up with modern-day demands. Ulysses' youngest son, Clarence, worked at Forbush's Market once Edenville was founded. The store received a lot of business, but saw its last day, too. When the new Pine Valley Marketplace was built, Forbush's Market, the first filling station, and the old feed store in Edenville, were torn down for the new development, which included the Hillview Apartments. Clarence, by that time, had devised plans to open a suitcase factory across the new highway. Another McGrew then became the first store manager at the brand new supermarket.

The valley's one-hundred years of history was not only about buildings and roads or storekeepers and postmasters. Tales filled the evenings around backyard barbecues. Memories were shared while hair styling in the beauty parlor. Funny stories were told around a scrap album where photos brought loved ones near. Even the night air rang with music and singing as old-time songs drifted from homes, accompanied by pianos and guitars. The best tales never made it into the essay contest. They were held close and carried in the heart. These stories involved the lives of those once loved, but who were sadly lost. Out of the bitter sweetness of painful memories and joyful recollections, ordinary townsfolk found peace while honoring their ancestors' lives lived well and with kindly purpose.

CHAPTER TWENTY-FOUR

The idea of writing about her family's role in settling the valley had enthralled Candelaria Hart. Yet, she did nothing about it. She loved remembering her grandparents, her uncles, and their many stories. They had lived there once, but were gone. Even her father was gone and her husband. Both of them were part of the past now. With her mother becoming old and needing her help, she believed it was best to disregard the essay contest. Work and taking care of her mother took up most of her time. To do more than that, she reasoned, would have been too much for her. So, she talked herself into letting it go.

This decision had the unfortunate result of infuriating her. She fumed at work, which annoyed her coworkers and led to a reprimand from the foreman. At home, she banged cupboards and drawers in the kitchen out of her frustration. In town, she avoided others until her daughter mentioned having seen her in public.

They were at home in the farmworkers housing, Villa Borracho. Candelaria was changing out of her work clothes and getting ready to take a bath. Rosa was in the kitchen preparing dinner.

She said, "I saw you in town, Mom. You were acting like you had a black eye you didn't want anyone to see."

Tying her robe, Candelaria came into the kitchen and asked, "What are you talking about?"

"The way you were acting," Rosa said. She took some plates out of the cupboard and set them on the counter before saying, "You were turning away from people on the sidewalk, hiding your face. What are you, a movie star now? What's going on?"

"Nothing's going on!" said Candelaria.

She left the room in a huff. Dropping her hairbrush on the bathroom floor, she bumped her head on the edge of the sink when she bent down to get it. Raising her voice, she said, "It's this silly contest. It has everyone acting like they think they're special, or something." Rubbing her head, she threw the brush into the sink.

Rosa was stunned, wondering whether to continue arguing or let it go. However, she wanted to have the last word in the matter.

She went into her mother's bedroom and said, "All I'm saying is, you were acting funny. I noticed people were looking at you, like they thought you were behaving strangely, too. It doesn't really matter to me. I just thought you'd like to know." She turned away from her mother and went back into the kitchen.

Candelaria closed the bathroom door and ran the bath water, ashamed of her anger and embarrassed. Disappointed in herself, she regretted letting anything get in the way of her entering the contest, an opportunity she honestly loved. The real reason she avoided participating could be seen beneath her decades-long struggle with anger. She was made uncomfortably aware of it at work during a meeting she had attended. A long-standing fact surfaced once again that farmworkers were treated unfairly simply because they were poor, disadvantaged, and predominately brown-skinned. She admitted to herself that she was ashamed, because, no matter how much the subject set her off, she told herself not to get involved. The struggle left her exhausted. She escaped to her usual state of depression.

Whereas Candelaria was not yet ready to face her past, Rosa thought about it often, particularly regarding the treatment they received for being Mexican. She felt something between her and her friend, Dottie, a barrier of sorts. Whether a sense of unwelcomeness or a feeling within herself, it made her try harder than everyone else, it seemed, simply to be equal in *their* eyes. Rosa wished to be seen for who she was on the inside.

Rosa knew that her brother was set apart from his peers, mostly when he was a boy. She wondered how it was for him as an adult, if he still experienced anything. The talk about farmworkers' rights also reached her ears. She saw on television what was going on in the country. It made her think, it made her feel and, in her heart, it made her care. It was when they were little children that it began for her and her brother. He was so cute, she recalled. Wanting to be liked by others, he was instead singled out, and not only because of his brown skin. He was clearly a unique person.

Rosa heated up a can of beef stew for her and her mother's dinner, standing over the stove, staring at it as she stirred. Returning to that time, nearly twenty-five years before, she recalled when it became known to their family how different her brother was compared to other children.

•   •   •

Hearing the shouting of boys and their taunting words, Rosalita jumped off the swing and ran to her brother who was bent over by a bush. She pushed her way through the crowd of kids gathered around Little Jimmy and yelled at them to get away.

"Leave my brother alone!" she said. "Can't you see he's sick?!"

One of the boys began teasing her brother about having eaten too many chili peppers, a rude slur for being Mexican. Never mind their father was of English ancestry. Little Jimmy's darker brown skin at that stage in his life, told others he was only Mexican, as though that were something shameful.

Rosalita ignored them as she took care of her seven-year-old brother. Soon, the other children lost interest and dispersed. Little Jimmy felt weak and needed to go home. Rosalita brought him to the bathroom first to wash his hands and face. Afterward, wrapping her arm around him, she led him away from the school. They were both hurt by the experience, saddened and dejected, Little Jimmy especially. It was his first year of school being on the playground with the older children. His hair had gone uncut for some months and his parents had not provided him with new clothes. He came to school in torn and stained ones and was further singled out for his skin color, getting cruelly teased. It was more than he could bear.

Rosalita knew they should have stayed at school, but she was angry that none of the grown-ups bothered to help. She cared less about the rules because of that. What mattered to her was protecting her brother and taking care of him. So, away from the school they turned to walk the two-mile distance homeward.

Her brother was quiet. They needed to stop once more along the way for him to get sick again. Soon, he began to talk.

"Why did they have to be so mean to me, Rosalita?"

"Oh, never mind those kids, Jimmy. They were just being stupid."

"But, why? I never did anything to them."

Rosalita knew better and asked him, "Why are you mean to me sometimes?"

"When I'm mad?"

"Yeah. Maybe those kids were mad about something else."

"Oh. Maybe they have a Mean Uncle, too?"

Rosalita smiled at the thought of this, happy that maybe the other kids also had a tough time of it, not disliking them so much. She forgot her anger and agreed with her brother.

"Yeah. Maybe they have a Mean Uncle, too," she said.

Having settled that, she placed her arm around him, trying to think up something to boost his spirits.

She sang, "There was a farmer had a dog and Bingo was his name-o. B-I-N-G-O!"

"I'm tired," he complained.

"We're almost there. B-I-N-G-O!"

"It's too far!" Little Jimmy said.

The grass along the sides of the road was tall. Little Jimmy could only see what lay straight ahead. The roof of their house appeared far away in the distance.

"We'll just go to the barn," said Rosa. "Maybe Daddy's there and can give us a ride home."

By the time they reached the barn, their spirits lifted, especially once they saw their father. He got one look at his poor son looking all woebegone, hair past his shoulders which, out of his own guilt, led him to chastise his wife at home.

"Look at the poor boy, Larie! Don't you think you oughta cut his hair, at least? And when was the last time he got a decent pair of shoes and some pants? No wonder he's sick, like some forgotten hobo's child. That's what he looks like!"

However, Candelaria did not need the chastising. She was pregnant and struggling with morning sickness which, in her case, was all-day sickness. She felt badly enough all by herself, and brooded over the fact, because she had not yet told her husband. It could wait, she thought. She had Little Jimmy take a bath and lie down in bed, telling him he was getting a haircut regardless of whether he wanted one, for it was his own choice to let his hair grow.

"No," he weakly argued with his mother. "I wanna grow my hair long like Uncle Dexter."

His father stepped into the room at that statement and asked, "Uncle Dexter? What do you want long hair like that for?"

He tearfully answered, "I wanna braid my hair like him and wear six-guns, so I can mow down any kid at school who makes fun of me."

Little Jimmy's weak body sank into his bed. A blanket was draped over him and a kiss planted on his feverish forehead by his mother.

Big Jimmy, trying not to laugh at his son's reasoning, said, "Well, even Uncle Dexter knows it's time to stop totin' six-guns and get along with everybody."

Candelaria sent Rosalita to her grandparent's to ask them if any of her cousins had outgrown their clothes and shoes. Rosalita returned with her Grandma Ev, carrying a big stack of clothes and some shoes for herself and for Little Jimmy.

Little Jimmy had a better go of it once he was well enough to return to school. Big Jimmy went along with him to speak to the principal, chiding the man for allowing such a thing as his son being teased when he was getting sick in the bushes. While he was at it, he slung out one last reprimand. It made him feel less guilty for having been a neglectful father and more sympathetic of his son's situation.

"Now, I hope this ain't gonna happen again!" he shouted at the principal. "This is the only son I got and I'd like to see him grow up all in one piece."

Apologies and reassurances were given that it would never happen again. It did happen again, so Big Jimmy decided, without telling his wife, that he would privately teach his son a few punches. It only served to single out the boy even more, branding him a trouble-maker.

Rosalita and Candelaria were at a loss over what to do regarding Little Jimmy. He exhibited a mysterious boost in confidence and a voracious appetite for using his fists to settle arguments. Little Jimmy had an answer for that when they asked him about it. His dad had taught him what to say to those kids or anyone who dared make fun of him again.

Standing tall, with fists readied, he would say, "Come here and say that!" Another one, he said with hands on his hips and a squinty-eyed, tough-guy look on his face. "Get ready, cuz I'm gonna feed you my fist!"

Then, there was his very best one he made up himself, which his dad assured him was a real good one. It was a special one saved for the extra-tough kids he might have to catch off guard before he let them have it.

Rosalita, spying on them from a knothole in the barn wall one day, saw Little Jimmy and their father practicing fighting. Her brother held his hand up and said, "Wait a minute." He then waved their dad over toward him, saying, "Come here. I wanna tell you a secret." Caught off guard, their dad dropped his arms and relaxed, asking Little Jimmy, "What?" Right then, Little Jimmy plowed into him, knocking him down. In a hurry, Rosalita was off and running to inform their mother.

"Leave them be, Rosalita," said Candelaria. "Your father's right. Your brother needs to learn how to defend himself."

To which the girl breathed in and let out a loud and groaning sigh over her hopeless parents as she walked away. "Okay," she warned, "don't blame me if he comes home with a note from the principal."

Even Walter Henry tried to reason with Big Jimmy. "I don't know if teaching the little scrapper to fight is such a good idea," he said.

Their visits to the principal's office grew in number, exactly as Rosalita had warned. Clearly, Big Jimmy only made matters worse.

It was Candelaria's turn to chastise her husband. With their new baby in her arms, she asked, "Do you want both of our sons to be troublemakers?"

If there was one thing Big Jimmy did not want to eat, it was crow. He finally learned his lesson. It may have been funny to see his son acting tough, and he may have believed it was his job as a father to teach his son to fight, but he realized he never bothered to understand what his son was up against. He got a taste of it, no less unpalatable than the proverbial crow.

He was in the livery stable one afternoon and heard his son up in the loft, crying. It was his son's hiding place. Big Jimmy climbed up the rungs of the ladder to see the boy curled up in a ball, crying and sniffling.

"Hey, come 'ere, Son," he said.

They climbed down from the loft and Big Jimmy picked up the boy to comfort him. The things his own father used to teach him and his brothers how to be a man and get along in the world did not work with his own son. He realized that. He dusted off his son's pants, swept the hay from his hair and his shirt, and saddled up Theodore. He placed his son on the saddle and then mounted the horse. They rode to Forbush's Market for an ice cream soda that may have only cost two bits for both of them to have one, but that was a precious quarter, indeed, which Little Jimmy could appreciate.

"Thanks, Dad," he told his father.

They sat at the counter, when in walked the inseparable trio, Tucker James Stewart, Sylvia Cadwallader, and Forty Sumner, who received plenty of teasing at school, himself. His round belly always poked out from the bottom of his undersized t-shirts.

Trying not to get involved in matters, Big Jimmy could not help but observe what took place next. He soon discovered the source of his son's tears. It was the cute, five-year-old girl with gray eyes. His son would not take his eyes off her. Little Jimmy had the most forlorn look, perking up a bit to say to her, "Hi, Syl," with such a sweetness to it.

His hopefulness was rewarded by her response, spoken in an equally sweet voice. "Hi, Jimmy," she said.

Tucker James got his friends rounded up and said, "Let's get out of here," which brought Big Jimmy to realize whatever was going on was not cute, nor was it funny.

He knew, all in one piece, why his son was being picked on at school, why the boy fought so relentlessly, and pretty much did not have a single friend to call his own in that town. It was because he was a threat. Not an ordinary threat, but a huge threat to all the nice people who tried to get everyone to live like them, look like them, talk like them, and think like them. All the goodly folk in their look-alike houses on their look-alike streets, where everything was supposed to appear so perfect and orderly, were threatened by a little boy who could not nor would not conform to their ways.

Looking at his son, who had a squished wad of dog turd poking out from the bottom of his boot, having lodged itself there, and who was oblivious to his dusty, dirty clothes, while happily shoveling ice cream into his grimy face, it brought such joy to Big Jimmy. But, it also broke his heart, for nothing short of "wild" could describe his cherished boy. A wild child was never going to be a part of things in that town.

Big Jimmy's blood ran cold, for in his own heart there stirred the wildness of his forebear's, namely his grandfather, Josiah, a man who could not fit in with a town determined to become civilized and domesticated. Not having considered his son's native heritage in his brief assessment, Big Jimmy nevertheless saw that his son had a hell of a life ahead of him and one long hell of a fight, too. He knew if his son ever gave in or gave up, he would be as good as dead. From time to time, Big Jimmy was painfully reminded of this truth. His son was not one to follow along with the others, but to go his own way, everyone else be damned, or he would suffer a grievous sickness of his very soul.

Many was the time that Rosalita stepped in to protect her brother. Many was the time he disappeared only to be found up in the loft in tears. The boy's wild heart at least found some solace in what his mother and his Grandpa Jesse taught him. Whereas Candelaria taught her son many ways to cope, Grandpa Jesse saw in the boy something of his own father, Berto Mendoza. He told Little Jimmy and Rosalita about their great-grandparents, Berto and Lucy, while they sat together during their many campfire nights of marshmallow roasting and popcorn popping. Little Jimmy loved these times and wanted to be like his grandfather's family. Jesse wanted his grandson to know Berto and Lucy and their peaceful ways, something he knew the boy had within him, but needed help expressing.

Candelaria's parents, her grandmother, and even she and her husband could say all they wanted and do all they could, but, in the end, it would be up to Little Jimmy Hart, himself, whether he would apply it and, so, benefit from their teachings. However, what they failed to see, Walter Henry and his sister, Lulabelle, did not miss. A little bit of Josiah Hart, like a coarse, black pebble, dwelled restlessly within Little Jimmy's soul. Grinding away at his core as he grew up, it had more power than all their words combined.

•   •   •

Bringing her mind back on the present, Rosa spooned the beef stew into two bowls and set them on the table. She cut up some lettuce for a salad, then buttered a few slices of bread. When she called her mother to say dinner was ready, Candelaria walked out of her bedroom and into the kitchen. Rosa noticed the angry expression on her mother's face. Turning aside, she stepped outside onto the front porch to gaze upon the last rays of sun departing from the day. Eyes glistening, she looked toward where her boyfriend lived, counting the days.

"Goodbye, Rosa Hart," she whispered. "Hello, Rosa Smith."

CHAPTER TWENTY-FIVE

Several years had passed since the essay contest. Candelaria had realized her dream of becoming a writer and worked very hard. She was in the public library one afternoon, getting ready to leave after typing up her latest story. Since it was closing time, the librarian also busied herself with briefly tidying her desktop.

When Candelaria was ready to go, she lingered nearby, her arms laden with notebooks and her heavy purse slung over her shoulder. She appreciated the friendship that had developed between herself and the librarian and hoped they could walk together after leaving the library.

In her usual, formal manner, she said to her friend, "Thank you, Miss Winters, for letting me use the typewriter."

"Call me Katie," said the librarian as she stood up from her chair behind her desk.

"Okay," Candelaria agreed.

Katie was encouraged by the friendly exchange between them. Since no one else was there besides them, she wanted to take advantage of what privacy the library afforded them and share something personal with Candelaria. Although, she grew anxious at the thought of what she planned to say.

"Uh, Larie?" she asked.

"Yes?" answered Candelaria.

Katie said, "I've been wanting to tell you something for a very long time now. I've been worried whether or not it was the right thing to do, but I've decided that keeping secrets is always wrong."

Candelaria's brow wrinkled and her mouth closed tightly. Her body stiffened. Though her heart was racing, she struggled to remain calm and listen. After all, she reminded herself, Katie was her friend.

"I've never told anyone," said Katie, "except Walter Henry and Sister Ruth." She placed the cover over the typewriter and stepped around her desk, asking, "Did you know that Johnny Henry is my son?"

Stunned, Candelaria could only think to say, "Oh? I had no idea." Although, she had heard the gossip and made her own observations over the years. She never discussed them with another person, though. In addition, that was years ago. Johnny was grown up and all of that was part of the past, she reasoned.

Katie unconsciously ran her fingertips along the edge of the desk as she said, "Yeah, he's my son. I came to work here, so I could be near him, be in his life somehow."

Candelaria began to see the issues of the past twenty years rise before her eyes. They were things she had merely kicked off the side of the road into a ditch, when no one was looking, only for them to crawl back out, having never gone away. Her son's marriage to Beth, his affair with Sylvia Sumner, and that little boy, so precious, appearing in Walter Henry's life, like a mystery, like...a secret...

She blurted out, "Oh, my God! Miss Winters! I-I mean, Katie. I don't know what to say. Have you told him? Johnny? Does he know? Surely, he must have suspected."

"Uh...I-I don't know," Katie answered. "I wanted to tell you first, before I give him a letter I wrote years ago for Walter Henry and Sister Ruth to give him. They never did."

Candelaria puzzled over why Katie would tell her first. She grew worried.

Katie feared saying any more than she already had. She became the young woman with scruffy hair again, cruelly rejected by her mother and expecting the same treatment from Candelaria. Yet, with voice trembling, she said, "The reason I wanted to-to tell you, is because the-the letter also tells, uh, Johnny about his-his father." Crying and shaking, she said, "His father is your son. Jim. He's Johnny's father."

Candelaria said, "No. No! That's not true!" She was not prepared for this. "Why are you saying these things? Why are you telling me this?!" she shouted.

"Because it's the truth," said Katie. "I need to tell my son the truth. I've denied him long enough! Please, Larie, I need you to know. You're his grandmother! Surely you—"

Candelaria exploded. "Stop it! Stop it! You're lying to me!" she said. "I don't want to hear this!"

She fled the library. Years of secrecy, denial, and looking the other way confronted her. Walking away from the school grounds, she saw no one, for she was off in another realm, a realm of altered realities, crossing dimensions to places where she had only begun to travel. Between the worlds, she stepped, not here, not there, but in-between, where her deepest, most profound secrets remained carefully tucked away. Her own pain, because of which she was unable to bear another's, yet still hold on to her own, was surfacing quickly.

Returning to the scene of the crime, the location of the wounding that was triggered, Candelaria became the girl child, lost and alone, fleeing the school in search of her parents. She was not on the earth, but floating above it, aloft on the wind, in the rays of the sun, in the songs of the birds, being carried where she knew not, until she had arrived.

She went home, like when she was a child, home to her parents, home to safety, to love, to acceptance, and to welcomeness. But, the house was no more. It had burned down long ago. She sat on its front door step. Legs drawn up close with her arms wrapped around them, she cried. The mountain winds swept down from the snowy crest far above, down into her life. Where it touched her, she felt terribly alone. Her husband had died, then, her mother. Sadly, her son died as well. Rosa married Buster Smith and moved in with him. A cousin came to live with her, which helped, but something was missing from her life. It needed her attention and, within that lonely feeling, she knew she would now do this. She needed to. She needed to face her pain she hid beneath a lifetime of rage.

Through her crying, she asked herself in a low voice, "Why am I so angry?" Fearing someone might hear her and know she was at last taking stock of a past she had wanted to keep buried, she whispered, "Why am I so angry?"

The tall elms would not reply, nor the fir or the pine trees growing thick, leaving remnants of her laughter to gather in the shadows of an absent home. It was her home, she realized, and it was gone, burned down. Its charred bones and gutted innards were carried off, leaving only the way into that old house. No doorway existed, nor any rooms where her mother and father danced to the music playing on their old victrola. Her big sister remained frozen in age, left behind, becoming younger and younger than Candelaria.

They said it was cancer. Her sister was too vibrant, too alive to be struck down so young. Candelaria buried her face into her knees and tried to be angry, but only tears ran, tears from a grief misplaced. She tried to get mad, but how could she strike out at those whom she loved? At God? At Death? No. Here, is when she ventured into the shadowy presence before her, held in abeyance for what was yet to come. She mustered her courage to face it.

Was she mad, because of the race of people to which she was born? She had never lived in Mexico. Her father had never lived there, nor her mother, nor Mama Stefa. Only through her grandfathers, Berto and Joaquin, could she make the connection to a land she had never seen. All she could relate to was who she was, brown, and yet, it was this color that betrayed her origins in Mexico and amongst the native people who once lived in Pine Valley.

The other children who saw her at school, saw only her brown skin. They called her names. Sylvia's mother, Charity, was among them. Someone pushed her down once and kicked the gravelly dirt on her. They spoke with such hatred, their faces pinched into a scowl intending to let her know she was but a thing to be despised, a foul and dirty thing that brought disgust to those who looked upon her. Uttering their curses, not out loud, but under their breath, ensured their hurtful words would only be for her. Although, her friend, Esther Chavez, told her she was also called names.

Boys would shout toward her on the playground at school, trying to get her attention. Esther would pull on her arm to drag her away from her anger left to lie on the blacktop of the basketball court, where she would find it again the next day.

"Dirty Mexican! Why don't you take a bath?!" others said to her.

The abuses continued into high school. The foul-mouthed ones had a permanent sneer from basically hating everyone, perhaps even themselves. They always had their fists in their pockets, their smokes gripped in their hands to draw out and pop a cigarette into the corner of their mouths after their expletives were spewed across the road.

Candelaria and Esther would stiffen in fear, hurriedly walking homeward, hoping they would not be followed and accosted again like once before. The young men had encircled them that time, grabbing their purses away and knocking their books onto the ground as they taunted Candelaria and Esther.

"Why don't you go back to Mexico where you belong?!" the young men yelled at them.

The words meant nothing to Candelaria except for the way they were said. They were intended to be mean, to inflict harm, a barb, a thrust, a wounding to knock her down to the very dirt beneath their shoes. She was wounded so many times by their weapons of hate that she, like her son, bore the scars she spent a lifetime hiding under long-sleeved shirts. So, she worked only with the other Mexicans, the other ones whose brown skin told everyone they were different. They were different. That's all. They were different.

She avoided people in town except those who talked to her first in a kind way, who were respectful and treated her as simply a person, not a brown-skinned person, not a Mexican or a native person, but simply as herself. She had feared becoming a writer and then to share what she had written with others, feared sending her writing in to be published, to put herself out there specifically to tell her story, all because of that. Avoiding any discussion about it, she feared others would think of her as racist, that she was ashamed of being Mexican. Candelaria admitted she was ashamed, but only for her unwillingness to examine why. She was ashamed, because she never stood up to her attackers back then when she wanted to, to fight them, to say out loud, "Hey! My name is Candelaria!"

•　　•　　•

The wind died down and the evening quieted. Candelaria saw her notebooks lying where she had dropped them. She reached inside her purse for some tissue to wipe her eyes and her nose. The memories of the past seemed to have cleared. She was growing calm, quieting within herself, although the sorrow of her remembrances lingered in her heart. Nevertheless, it was getting dark. She needed to go home, so began walking up the driveway toward the road. Before she left its sight, she turned around to look back at a house that was only in her memory. Tears streamed down her face again, but they were tears of love, of release, of knowing truth. Those days were long gone, she told herself. She was free. She was finally free.

Candelaria's life, for so many years, was ruled by suffering. How she wanted to let those days drift away like the leaves on the wind. All she wanted to do was to laugh and smile.

"No more suffering," she told herself. "It's time to rejoice."

Awakening to her gifts, she believed, was but the beginning. This day, it dawned on her, she was awakening once more, this time to joy. She felt it stirring in her heart, felt its energy rising upward within herself, bringing her into a new way of being. She was not alone. Her life had merely changed. So much promise awaited her, in her writing...and in learning about Jim's son, Johnny. She laughed at the wonder of it. Oh, if her mother was alive, they would dance, she thought. Thrilled at the very idea of dancing, Candelaria set down her notebooks and purse and, in the approaching night, she danced. All by herself, Candelaria danced.

CHAPTER TWENTY-SIX

The open fields below were yet green in that early summer, the orchards in full leaf, but it was the surrounding trees that struck Johnny Henry so profoundly. He got out of his truck and stood, admiring the conifers growing densely throughout Pine Way and upon the hills beyond, wondering why he ever left. It was so beautiful to him and he felt as he had when only a boy, when Walter Henry first brought him there to live with them. Everything appeared larger than life, more colorful, more richly imbued with something he could not name that impassioned and inspired him. Feeling a tinge of sadness as he looked on, he could not help but smile, because he was home. Johnny knew he had made the right choice. He came home.

He had left town soon after his high school graduation, believing he would never return. But, after two years of college, he was pulling the horse trailer across the small valley once more, reveling in the familiar sights of Edenville and Pine Way. Arriving at the cabin, he grew anxious and unsure. He parked the truck at their small horse barn and caught sight of the striking view from his truck window.

Walter Henry had passed away the year before after a brief illness. That was 1971, when Johnny found himself the sole heir to their house and wood shop, Lulabelle's retreat center, and the decrepit old blacksmith shop and livery stable. Returning home to the loss of family that took place in his absence, Johnny experienced the peacefulness of that healing place upon the mountainside, but he also felt a nudge from within himself that told him to share it with others.

"I ain't gonna ask her," he said to the walls one night while lighting the kerosene lantern. "I'd rather jump off a cliff than talk to her."

He argued with himself, "She dumped me! Didn't even want me, the—"

Every day, he busied himself with chores that never seemed to end, but this eventually proved impossible for reasons he yet tried to avoid. Talking to himself one lonely evening as he scraped the last of the Spaghetti-O's from a can he had heated on the stove, he agreed with himself, "Well, I probably ought to go and talk to her."

The Edenville Elementary School librarian, Miss Winters, whom Johnny suspected was his mother since he became a teenager, had given him a letter the first time he visited her at the school after returning home. Sharing with her his plans to stay, brought a big smile to her face, he recalled.

Johnny had waited to read the letter until he was back at the cabin. Her handwriting was familiar, because he had known her all his life. She was the woman in his dreams of a mysterious life lived he knew not where. She was the one woman in town who had been his favorite "lady person," something which he had shared with Jim Hart, his real father. Though he had known for several years, Johnny never asked Jim if he was aware that Miss

Winters was his mother. Reading the letter, however, changed things. He was no longer a boy, an innocent, but a grown man. The reality of what she had done to him, abandoning him to strangers, was sinking in and he was shocked by her actions, saying to himself, "I can't believe she did that!"

Stirred up and angry, he wanted to return to the school that same day, but it was late, so he waited to go the next day. However, months went by until, at the start of the following school year, he finally opened the door to the public library, stepped in, and saw her, the woman who gave him to Walter Henry. How many times had he walked through that door, not knowing she was his mother? How many times had he felt compelled to go to the library only so he could be close to this woman? The boy that he was, yet lived within himself as he experienced the painful truth re-awakening in his heart.

Seated at her desk with reading glasses and jewel-bedecked necklace, sat his mother, Miss Winters, Miss Katherine Winters, and Johnny felt himself falter. He wanted to turn around and leave before she saw him standing by the door, but he was unable to leave and, so, did nothing except wait for her.

She handed a book to a patron. When they turned to walk toward the door, she saw him. Without hesitating, he hurried toward her, almost at a run, as she leapt from her chair. They embraced, holding one another as if for the first time after a long separation. Tears and laughter of overwhelming joy streamed down their faces and into their hearts, as though it were light from heaven above. Down it poured into the well of lost years, filling it with hope, with wholeness and completion, with truth and with love.

Despite Johnny's misgivings, he said, "All these years...I've known for years...and I couldn't say a word to you. Why couldn't

I? Why not? It hurt so much!" Feeling himself becoming angry again, his mother spoke.

"So many times, I wanted to tell you," she said. "I wanted to tell the Henry's that I changed my mind and decided to raise you, but—" Her head dropped and she wept, shaking her head at the futility of her attempt to explain the past, the problems she had and the struggle to overcome them. "Please, forgive me!" she said.

Johnny looked away from her as though in thought, turning his head down, unable to face her. "I just want us to be able to talk about it," he said, lifting his head to look into her eyes. Raising his voice, though not in anger, he added, "I want to be able to tell the whole world you're my mother!"

"I do, too," she said as she wiped her eyes with a tissue. "But, how will we do that...in this town?"

"I know where we can start," said Johnny. "C'mon, I'll show you," and he turned to leave.

Katie grabbed her purse and sweater, then followed him out the door, locking it behind. "Where are we going?" she asked.

"You'll see," he said.

They left the school and walked to the cemetery. When they reached it, they stepped through the wrought-iron gate made by Johnny's great-grandfather, Timothy. Candelaria was there, placing flowers on someone's grave.

Katie hesitated and glanced at her son.

He let go of his mother's hand and instead placed his arm around her and said, "I need to do this."

Johnny had seen Candelaria entering the cemetery on his way to the library. He wanted her to be the first person he would tell and he wanted his mother with him when he told her.

He addressed Candelaria. "Um...Mrs. Hart?" he asked.

Startled, she turned her head to look their way.

Determined, Johnny approached her and said, "I'd like for you to meet my mother, Miss Katherine Winters."

Candelaria began to smile, but, still feeling remorseful over her past behavior, she humbly replied, "Yes, yes, I know. Your mother told me."

She stepped closer to Johnny and gently hugged him. "You're my grandson," she said. You're my grandson!"

Candelaria also hugged Katie, apologizing to her for the lost years. "I'm so sorry," she said, "for getting so angry with you when you told me. I should have done something, back when I first suspected Johnny was Jim's son. I should have!"

"You don't have to apologize," Katie said. "I shouldn't have kept it secret. It was a mistake."

Candelaria grasped their hands and, lifting them in the air, announced, "We're family!" She laughed and said it again, "We're family!"

She looked into her grandson's eyes for the very first time. She saw the baby boy that he was who came to their town to live, the toddler who rode in the truck with Jim, the boy who ran into the church to stand next to his father, and the young man who placed Jim's football medal on his coffin and called him a hero.

Caressing his face and brushing the hair from his forehead, she said, "I love you, Johnny. I've been wanting to tell you that for a very long time."

She placed her arms around him in a loving embrace, laughing and crying at the same time, for her laughter had come home to her heart. Feeling lighter and more at peace, she affectionately tousled his hair.

The three of them gathered close to one another and stood before the grave of a man no one could say they understood, but all could say they loved. The inscription on the headstone read, "James Henry Hart, born 1934, died 1967. Son~Husband~Friend. *He was our hero.*"

Katie added, "And father, too. Right, Johnny?"

She placed her arm around her son, so that all three stood arm in arm, facing the headstone. Candelaria was the tallest, at five-feet-five-inches-tall, then Johnny, at five-feet-four-inches, and Katie, who was barely five-feet-tall. They had known one another for nearly two decades, forging a bond of friendship and love. The truth of their relationships silently waited in the wings for its chance to take center stage. It released them to love freely and openly as they had been longing to do for many years.

Candelaria could remember how she felt when she saw little Johnny riding in the truck with his dad and Walter Henry. There was a deep need in her to have that child in her life as well. She remembered seeing him walking by her shack, and so many times have the urge to say to him, "Hi, Johnny!" Yet, she only did so on one occasion before he left for college. So many regrets, too many to continue holding on to, so she decided to hold on to the joy and laughter instead.

Candelaria's daughter, Rosa Smith, drove away from the school where she worked as a teacher. She was on her way to her mother's, having some good news of her own to share. She wanted to tell her mother that she and Buster decided it was time to move to a bigger house, since she was expecting her third child. Spotting her mother at the cemetery, she drove down Peach Tree Lane to the cemetery beyond St. Peter's Catholic Church. Her mother was standing near the front gate, talking and laughing with Miss Winters and Johnny, whom Rosa knew well. Her mother looked so different, happy and excited, smiling and animated.

When Rosa parked and got out of her car, her mother hurried toward her, shouting, "Rosa! Rosa! You're not going to believe it!" She embraced Rosa with such an energy, it took her by surprise. With her mother's arm around her waist, she was led over to Miss Winters and Johnny. She listened to the story. Looking first at Katie and then at Johnny, she was dumbfounded, because she had no idea. She was almost disbelieving what she heard, yet was struck with astonishment, eager to know more.

Teasing, she said, "Miss Winters, huh?" Playfully, she held her index finger out to say with a grin, "So, you're the reason my brother spent so much time out in the woods that summer. I knew something was going on, but I had no idea what it was!" She added in wide-eyed glee, "I even saw you two heading up the trail together that goes to the Henry's. That was you!" She turned away and back, feigning incredulity, rolling her eyes, and placing her palm on her cheek, saying, "That was you! All these years."

She lovingly hugged Johnny, the sad boy she had hugged before in the diner one day long ago. Privately, she was overtaken with compassion for him. Out of everyone involved, it was he who was, undoubtedly, hurt the most by what never should have been kept a secret. How they would have handled it then, she dared not guess, but certainly having the truth out from the start would have been better. She thought about their uptight town, where no differences, no improprieties were allowed, yet took place beneath everyone's noses, regardless. She learned from her students that all sorts of unpleasantries visited upon those who lived in nice houses as frequently as those who lived in old, wooden shacks. It was for this sole reason, she felt sad for Johnny. The situation was not faced openly, simply because it was considered shameful.

Rosa decided to hold off telling her mother her own good news until later. She hugged Katie and said, "Welcome to the family. Both of you. It's been a long time coming."

Her children were with her in-law's, so she was pressed for time, unable to think of anything more to say. It was so new and overwhelming.

They briefly lingered, agreeing to get together for dinner or a picnic to talk some more. Two decades of secrecy and denial could not be taken lightly. Candelaria walked back to her son's grave, Rosa drove away, and Johnny walked back to the school to get his truck.

Katie remained standing outside the gate to the cemetery. She watched her friend stand beside the grave of the man she had loved and lost. Feeling like that troubled young woman again, she entered the cemetery and approached Candelaria. She said as though to herself, "It was a long time ago."

Candelaria quickly glanced behind her, smiling. She reached her arm out to Katie, asking, "Stand here with me?"

That special summer between Jim Hart and Katie Winters would be held sacred in Katie's heart. Yet, she wanted Jim's mother to know, "he was a peaceful man, a loving man." Becoming silent again, her heart experienced its youthful desire for him. The day she and Jim met one another again in the woods, and she said goodbye to him, only to turn and watch him walk away, appeared in her memory.

"I loved him," she said.

That night, as Candelaria lay in her bed in the old shack in Villa Borracho, she dreamed of building her own house, how it would look, where she would have it built. She dozed, listening to the sounds of the night outside her bedroom window. Crickets had begun their chorus and the clicking of bats swooping through the trees was audible to her as she drifted off to sleep. Feeling as though she were already in her new home, she began to remember her dream in which an angel told her something important.

The angel said, "The day will come when you will see the sun arise. You will learn the true meaning of joy. Life's mystery shall unfold for you."

Candelaria thought of her grandson, Johnny, realizing the gift that was given to them. Her tears burned as she said, "Oh, Jim! How I wish you were still here. I miss you!"

CHAPTER TWENTY-SEVEN

John James Henry was only a boy when he first came to Edenville. Less than two years of age, he watched as his mother prepared for their trip that day. He stood by the sofa in the apartment they shared with her friends as she gathered his toys, his clothes, and his diapers, setting them in a pile by the front door. All he remembered of that particular day, were his mother's legs as she walked back and forth across the living room. She was upset about something, talking to herself in her haste, before picking him up and carrying him out to the car.

"All right, little man," she said. "Time to meet your daddy."

The drive from the small town where they lived was but a few miles, but he fell asleep on the back seat of the car. When she turned left, his body slid across the seat toward one side of the car. When she swung her car to the right, he again slid across the vinyl seat cover toward the other side of the car. She was oblivious, eyes staring straight ahead at the road, occasionally scratching her scalp or chewing on a fingernail. If anyone were to say what they witnessed when Katie Winters drove past, their words might be, "Did you see that? That little, itty bitty woman just drove on past the stop sign!"

He awoke when they arrived in Edenville, noticing his mother was not in the car. He sat up and climbed between the bucket seats to stand behind the steering wheel. Johnny loved pretending he was driving the car. Whipping that steering wheel one way and then another, he filled his diaper, pounded on the horn, and giggled. When his mother came out of a store and hurried over to the car, he began telling her all about his own trip driving. She evidently misunderstood him, because she ignored every word, which was spoken in his own language.

After she changed his diaper, they drove off again. Johnny was scared. It reminded him of when his mother went to work and he was left with her friends. Each time, he waited anxiously until she returned. But, this time felt different. His anxiety grew as they approached Pine Way. She turned right and parked the car at an enormous and truly wondrous building. It was the blacksmith shop and livery stable. Johnny was in awe. He loved it and thrilled when his mother picked him up and carried him inside.

He was handed over to Walter Henry, along with all his possessions. His mother drove away without saying goodbye or even looking back at him one last time. He felt safe in Walter Henry's arms. Even though he could not have known that would be the last time he saw his mother, until after she moved to Edenville, he accepted things as they had presented themselves. When Jim Hart came walking up to the barn, Johnny knew all at once what had taken place. His mother said it was time for him to meet his daddy and that is what Johnny believed was taking place. The tall man approaching the barn was him.

From that time forward, Johnny loved and respected his father, feeling welcomed and, above all, wanted. Where his mother was concerned, he had felt unwanted, in the way, and a burden. With his father, there at the great big barn, he felt as though he had come home. When he was with his dad, all was right with the world.

Difficult days were present, certainly, but through it all, he looked to Jim for reassurance that everything would be okay. Jim was his hero, from the very first day they met until the last, when Johnny said his goodbyes at Jim's funeral thirteen years later. Walter Henry took care of him and loved him like a son, but no one could deny that Johnny needed his real father's love as well.

• • •

Grown up, with both his adoptive father and his real father gone from the world, Johnny drove into old Pine Way. Stopping in front of the barn, he parked his truck, which had the farrier's trailer hitched behind. It was morning and he was going to his first horseshoeing appointment. It felt natural to begin where both his dads worked for years, and their fathers, too. He opened the wide doors and entered the large structure, like an empty shell to him, too fragile to hope, yet too precious to let fall away. Hearing again the voices, the talk about horses, he recalled the sharp, sour smell of sweat and leather, the bite of smoke and sparks flying as hot coals were disturbed.

Johnny grew up within its rustic walls to the sounds and smells of horses always present. The tinkering and hammering at the forge as a horseshoe was carefully shaped, and the low whoosh of the bellows drawn down to blow upon the coals glowing brightly, were memorable sounds. He could still see Walter Henry standing by the forge, his heavy apron on over his worn overalls. Jim would have been busy cleaning the stalls or taking care of the horses. He and Walter Henry might engage in some light banter about work or their day. But, horses were no longer there, nor would there ever be again. The sharp clink and clank of iron being pounded was silenced the day Walter Henry died.

Johnny remembered something and turned to go back toward the door where a broken piece of mirror yet sat propped on a small shelf. Remembering when he had placed his treasures there so thoughtfully, he picked up each one and carefully examined them, the brown china horse, the playing dice, and the marbles, plus a few square head nails. He peered through a clear blue marble, then set it back down. The last item he picked up was a pair of eyeglasses. He left everything as they were, but slipped the eyeglasses into his shirt pocket to give to his grandmother. Turning to glance across the interior of the barn one last time, he whispered, "goodbye," and, "thank you."

Voices echoed in remembrance, having swept into the barn like a gust of wind. It came in a rush of feeling, his father saying, "I'm proud of you, Johnny! Good job, Son!"

Johnny began to realize his strength and purpose while standing in the vacant old barn. He knew he would be a fine horseman and farrier. Reassured, he locked up the barn and, taking a few steps out into the middle of the dirt road, he looked up at the sign above the doorway, reading it aloud: "Hart and Henry Blacksmith Shop and Livery Stable."

In that instant, Johnny promised himself that not only would his father and Walter Henry never be forgotten, but that speck of a town called Pine Way would not be allowed to fade into ruin. He would see that it was properly honored and restored. He had the wooden plaque Henry Henry carved long ago. It was at the wood shop and, with some careful restoring work, it was ready to be installed in its place of honor for when the time came. His adoptive father had shown him the old photograph of the way station and, digging out the plaque, pointed out to Johnny the exact location on the building where his own father wanted it to be placed, but never got the chance. Walter Henry had wanted to do something with it, so Johnny planned to honor both their dreams.

•   •   •

Pine Way was but a short-lived town. The Way, on the other hand, still dwelt there in spirit, like Henry Henry knew it would. When he and his wife retired each night at the way station, donning their nightcaps, slipping off their house shoes, and settling into bed, she routinely fretted over what had yet to be done. Listing this and that project or chore, she would ask him how they would ever get it all done. How would they find their way out of debt for all they had borrowed?

One night, as he lay smiling lovingly upon the moon, marveling at its mystery, at all the mysteries that lived in the quiet places of their lives and in their hearts, Henrietta once again bemoaned, "How will we ever find the way, Henry?"

Without a penny to their name, without an ounce of strength left to bear their dreams along any further, he answered, "No worry, my love." Speaking softly, tenderly, he said, "No need to worry," because he knew, "everything will be all right. In the end, my darling, the Way will be found."

Drifting off to sleep, Henry Henry cherished his secret plan to place the plaque he so patiently carved, waiting for his and his wife's anniversary to unveil it. He memorized its sentiment, its poem, which read, "It is told that, long ago, there walked a Man of Peace. He wandered near and wandered far with Love and Truth to teach. 'Tis words He spoke and wounds He healed, but only few did see, the Beauty that His wisdom held, the Way, the Life, the Mystery."

CHAPTER TWENTY-EIGHT

Early one morning on the year of his death, Walter Henry left his cabin. It was barely dawn. Owls yet glided on silent wings between the forest trees. Their loud chorus of hoots added to the sense of dread the old man felt since he decided to fulfill a long-avoided task.

Driving down the hill from his cabin, he closed in on Pine Way Junction and turned off the headlights. Most of Pine Way's houses were abandoned, but he knew Tucker Stewart still lived there and wanted to avoid rousing "the snoop," as he put it. Employing an old trick he knew, he speeded up when he neared the turn, then shut off the engine to let the vehicle coast downhill, past Tucker's house. He planned to restart the truck where it came to a standstill.

However, Tucker had a fitful night's sleep. At the barn, the day before, Walter Henry told him the story about his father's murder. The argument between Henry Henry and Josiah Hart kept repeating itself in Tucker's mind. Giving up on sleep, he went outside to sit on the porch steps with a cup of instant coffee and a plain cake doughnut.

He marveled at Walter Henry's truck silently coasting past his house. Up in a flash, he tossed out his coffee and hastily set the mug on the porch. It fell in the dirt along with the doughnut. Running into his house, he threw off his pajamas and robe and tried to get his pants on without falling over. He pulled on a t-shirt and, forgetful in his hurry, slipped his feet back into his slippers. Out the door he ran, arms flying wildly and legs moving faster than they had in years. He neglected to bring Freckles, his German Shepherd. She was left alone in the house whining frantically at his hasty departure.

He reached the barn, breathing heavily after his mad dash, only then wondering what he had done. Regardless, he braced himself and entered the old livery stable. Peering into the darkness, he could hear the old man stumbling around, uttering profanities. He also heard the clanking of metal.

Hesitating saying anything, he ventured to ask, "Walter?"

The old man was muttering to himself, "Can't find nuthin' when I need it! How am I supposed to—oh, great! Now Mr. Nosey, himself's, here...got an audience...watchin' me make a fool o' myself!"

"Can I help?" asked Tucker.

By the time the sun's bright rays shone through the forest, Walter Henry emerged from the barn with a shovel in hand. Crossing the road, he dropped it on the ground, went over to his truck, and began pulling a heavy wooden sign out of the truck bed.

"I should've done this years ago when Lucy told me to!" said Walter Henry. "It's my fault Jim Hart's dead! It's my fault he suffered all them years! I can't let the same thing happen to Johnny, can I? Well, can I?"

Tucker rushed to help Walter Henry with the sign, setting it down in the road. The old man began to dig a hole beside it, but was unsuccessful. Without hesitation, Tucker took the shovel from him, saying, "Here, let me," and began digging with more gusto than the toothless old man had in him anymore. Tucker knew Walter Henry was planning to put the sign in, though had no idea what it said, maybe a for sale sign, he imagined. When the hole was deep enough, he picked up the sign and set the post in the hole.

Walter Henry took over and turned the sign the way it was supposed to go. He began pushing dirt in around it, weakening from the effort.

Tucker helped fill in and tamp the dirt around the signpost. He stood back to read the sign's wording. "Welcome...to...The Way," he said.

Walter Henry retrieved something from his truck cab and lit it with a match. He began singing a song, more of a chant. It was a song Lucy Shoseegan taught him when he was a boy, orphaned when he lost his father to murder and his mother to grief soon thereafter. He hoped he sang the song correctly, though barely remembered the dance Lucy had shown him, which was supposed to be Lulabelle's part. He never told his sister about it. It was all right, because he was moving with the spirits that gathered around.

Nearly exhausted, the old blacksmith cried out again, "My mother did a terrible thing and I—" He sobbed, his weary body barely moving by that time. The smoldering old sage bundle Lucy gave him for his mission filled the air with its pungent smoke. "I should've done this back then! I should've! I should've! Worst mistake I ever made!"

Tucker held the sight in reverence and in awe, sensing the movement of dancing spirits and the dead rising as disembodied light and shadow. The sun shone upon them and the birds sang in the treetops when the lingering spirits of the dead departed into the light of heaven. Tucker saw great white birds and angels fly in to receive them and carry them home. He realized he was witnessing a sacred ceremony to address the terrible thing of which Walter Henry had spoken, inflicted by Pine Way's founding mother, Henrietta Henry.

No one would fault Walter Henry for his long-avoided task. After all, he was only a boy at the time and had been newly orphaned. Severely weakened, he stood leaning against his truck, his arms folded on the hood. He barely had strength enough to stand, his head buried in untold regrets laid upon the very earth.

Tucker looked at the sign they had planted. He never saw it before, never knew it existed. Despite its few words, he kept reading them until the shop's tenants arrived. A strange feeling came over him. It was not from what he had witnessed nor from what he derived from the experience, but from an awareness that came over him, ever so slight. It awoke in his chest and moved upward to the top of his head. It came on the wafting odors of green horse dung and fresh piss in the corral, though no horses had been kept there for years. It came on the wind that blew stronger with each minute that passed, the birdsong resounding, and the scent of a thousand roses filling his senses. His awareness grew to include something profound as salty, burning tears fell from the eyes within himself, beholding Truth.

"My God!" he said.

He spoke aloud to no one, merely out of an important knowing. He looked around and saw Walter Henry seated outside the barn door on an old weathered chair. Freckles had been left at the house, so Tucker needed to return home. He placed the shovel inside the barn, pausing to observe the tenants busy checking their inventory and loading up their truck with sacks of feed and bales of hay. He noticed the barn had a decided lisp to its walls as though a big wind could come up and blow it over, toppling it in its surrender to Time.

For over one-hundred years, the barn had been at the center. Tucker reflected on what it meant to him, to his parents, his grandparents. They had traversed the land and its travails, bringing their hearts and their livelihoods with them. Because of that, he was there.

No children in his life existed to whom to pass this important legacy. He wanted there to be. So, on that very day, he changed his routine and went to the bakery for a cinnamon roll and a hot chocolate, for which he had a sudden craving. It was located next door to his favorite bookstore, "Read 'em and Weep," which, he was embarrassed to admit, specialized in romance novels.

Eileen Price about choked on her tea when none other than the gorgeous hunk of man she once dated, stepped into her bakery, Tucker Stewart.

Teapot full o' Whimsy made the best cinnamon rolls, in Tucker's opinion. Brown sugar, butter, and cinnamon filling, with a sprinkling of chopped pecans and a drizzle of glaze on top, he much preferred them to those sold at the supermarket, which were encrusted with a thick slab of frosting. He was glad he came, not only for the rolls, but to see Eileen.

After he placed his order, saying, "Yes, I'd like the roll warmed," he took a chance.

"Excuse me," he said.

Eileen looked up at him, eagerly awaiting what he had to say to her.

"Eileen, right?" he asked.

"Yes! Yes! That's me!" she said. "And, you're Tucker Stewart. We dated once." Her head bobbed to the side as she rolled her eyes. She wore her blond hair drawn up into a short pony tail.

Tucker laughed and, grinning facetiously, added, "I seem to recall that."

He sat at one of the tables, soon enjoying his warm roll and hot cocoa while he and Eileen got caught up on each other's lives. He learned that Trudy Price had retired, so her daughter, Eileen, had taken over the business. Eileen was still single, had never married, nor did she have children, like himself.

He asked her, "Would you like to have dinner with me sometime?"

"I'd love to!" she answered.

After work that day, Tucker returned to the old blacksmith shop and livery stable, this time with Freckles. He wanted no surprises on the floor again when he arrived at home. With camera in hand and allowing Freckles to run loose, Tucker took pictures of the barn.

The tenants were busy closing up for the day, informing Tucker, "Walt's not here. He went home early. Said he felt unwell."

They soon drove away, leaving Tucker alone. He paused for a moment, looking sidelong at the ground, though not seeing it. A fleeting sense of grief regarding the old man had come over him. He smiled, thankful for having known Walter Henry and for helping the aged blacksmith relieve a lifelong burden of guilt.

CHAPTER TWENTY-NINE

Tucker remained standing in front of the barn. Clouds steadily building throughout the day presented a dramatic scene, their skirting edges lit by the waning sunlight. Magenta and orange-gold glowed upon the barn, the trees and shrubs, even the ground. It were as if the mysterious, dying town had come to life, emerging timidly from out of the shadows. He recalled the feeling he had that morning after Walter Henry had completed the ceremony. It was only a sense of something, but it dogged him. It stalked him, until he could at last free it from its secret keep, there, in the very light and color of life appearing to grow more brilliant as the sun lowered in the sky.

Candelaria Hart came walking around the corner and saw Tucker standing in front of the barn. She was struck by the beauty of that sunset and, at the same time, caught off guard by Tucker's presence. Nevertheless, she continued walking on her way toward where he stood. He turned to greet her.

"Hello," he said.

"Hi," said Candelaria. Noticing the sign, she asked, "Who put the sign there?"

"Walter Henry and I," said Tucker.

"Oh," was all Candelaria said. Feeling awkward and nervous, she debated whether to say something else, but only came up with, "I was out for a walk. I hope I didn't disturb you."

"No, no, you didn't." He took a chance and mentioned, "I was just trying to figure out something."

"What's that?"

"Oh, a feeling, I guess." His hands were in his pockets, his shirt sleeves partially rolled up. He was wearing his father's old wrist watch.

Candelaria stood beside him, gazing upon the ever-deepening colors in the west. "I know what you mean," she said. "I've felt something here, too."

"You have?" he asked.

"Oh, yes. There's something about this place," she said.

They stood in silence for a few minutes before Tucker asked, "Do you have some time? I'd like to show you something."

"Sure," replied Candelaria. "What do you want to show me?"

He walked over to the newspaper office. Candelaria followed him. For some reason, she still felt compelled to say something.

He unlocked the door, its weather-worn and swollen wooden frame stuck and difficult to push open. But, he managed to work it free. It swung open with a bang and a rattle of everything old and dusty about the entire building.

"I've been going through the office to clean it up, uhh, believe it or not." He was immediately confronted with a cobweb dangling from the ceiling. "And, I found something you might be interested in."

After telling Freckles to lie down inside by the door, he led Candelaria up the creaking stairs. Ascending the narrow stairwell of the aged structure from a lost and near-forgotten time in both their lives, they tread cautiously.

Tucker felt a strong need to connect with the mother of the young man he believed he had failed. At the top of the stairs, momentarily forgetting why he brought her there, what he wanted to tell her for years came to the foreground.

He approached the front window and looked down at the road and across to the trees, like so many times years ago, and said, "Mrs. Hart...I-I'd like to ask you to forgive me. I'm sorry, but I was not a very good friend to your son. I should have been. I should have been a friend to Jim. I should have tried to be his friend."

Hearing this, Candelaria recalled that day in the woods when she saw Tucker and Sylvia together. She realized that the girl Tucker was with was the same girl in whose arms her son had later drowned his pain. Yes, she could forgive Tucker, but regretted that she never forgave her son.

"I was not a very good friend to him either," she confessed. She had tried too hard to make her son be somebody he was not and was never meant to be. "I forgive you," she added, wishing she could say the same to her son.

She walked across the room to join him in looking out the window. No longer could she see her old house. It had burned down and was but a collapsed and blackened heap in the weeds with brush overtaking it. The peak of its half-burned roof was barely visible through the trees. In the silence between herself and Tucker, Candelaria began to share her own unsaid thoughts, when he turned and went toward a large desk sitting against the side wall of the room. Shelving was built around it, nearly empty, except for a set of several, leather-bound journals he drew from their cubby hole.

Without hesitation, Candelaria approached Tucker.

"Tucker?" she asked.

He looked at her, availing himself to her apparent need to say something.

"Yes?"

"I never told you—"

She began to lose her grasp on what she knew she had waited too long to say.

Tucker set the booklets down. His facial expression changed, his eyes holding such deep feeling for her.

Encouraged, she said, "I never told you how sorry I was for your family when I heard the news of your mother's death." Her hand went up to place it on his arm, lightly grasping it, holding him in case he might bolt and run, before she said, "I had lost my two baby boys and we were already struggling with Jim's problems. I was so sad. Your family lost so much, your sister, your brothers in the war, and your mom, then Dewey."

Tucker looked at her like he had become a boy again, a very guilt-ridden boy peeking out from behind a tree he had wanted to climb, but was too small. He was hiding behind it when his mother called his name. Once he came into view, she dropped to the ground in her death. He never stopped believing he had killed his own mother with his disobedience.

"It wasn't your fault she died," said Candelaria. "I talked to her once, here, in front of this office, one day that I saw her. She came to give your dad the news the doctor had told her, that she had heart disease and only had so long to live. The doctor gave her medicine, but she wouldn't take it. I told her she should, but she wouldn't. Then, I heard she had died and your grandparents, too! Oh, Tucker, I'm so sorry! I told her to take the medicine, but she wouldn't! All I know, is that I've been needing to tell you, that it wasn't your fault she died. It was simply her time, and she knew it. She knew it."

Candelaria's strength left her as whatever power had filled her, drained itself from her. Her voice trailed off to a place of sadness she was used to, all her life.

Tucker hugged her, which felt so natural, remembering she had hugged him when he was a little boy with a bruised eye put there by her son. He was crying and she carried him all the way down the road to the newspaper office to hand him over to his father and apologize, explaining to his dad what her son had done.

"He's such a good boy," Candelaria had told Tucker's father before she left. "You and your wife must be very thankful to have such a wonderful child for your son."

She set him down and hugged him, a tender kiss placed upon his brow.

His father replied, "Yes, we are. My wife and I love him very much."

"Thank you," Tucker said again to Candelaria, for both times she spoke up for him. "I appreciate you telling me that," he added.

He handed her the journals. "I think you might like to take these home," he said. "They'll just get thrown out or end up in the wrong hands."

"Whose are these?" she asked as she took the old and worn books from him.

"Herman left them here," he said. "He was your uncle, wasn't he?"

"Yes, yes, he was," said Candelaria.

She flipped through some of the pages to see they contained history, notes on his stay in Mexico, sketches, and poetry. Three of the volumes were from her grandfather, Berto Mendoza. Her Uncle Herman apparently had acquired them upon his father's death.

Candelaria was in awe. "Thank you!" she exclaimed. "Thank you, so much, for-for thinking of me to give these to. I didn't know very much about my uncle, or my grandfather. Maybe these will help me get to know them."

Tucker had browsed through them, mostly in Spanish, but there was enough in English for him to gather why Herman Mendoza never married. It took many years and a lot of growing up before Tucker realized his brother, Dewey, was of a similar persuasion. He knew these notebooks could not be left to lie. Herman, like his brother, Dewey, would not have wanted anyone to discover his secret. But, they helped Tucker to understand the woman beside him, for whom he felt so much love, missing Jim Hart all the more.

Like a boy receiving long-awaited comfort and forgiveness, Tucker accepted an impromptu hug from Candelaria.

"I miss him, too," she said, referring to her son, Jim.

Freckles was whining and whimpering, so they went down the stairs and out the door. Once Tucker got the door wrestled shut, he said, "Well, I guess it's time to get home. Good night. And, thank you, for everything." With Freckles happily trotting alongside, he walked away, waving to Candelaria.

Since it was late, Candelaria decided to go home.

Tucker stopped and called out, "Mrs. Hart?"

Her arms laden with the stack of journals, Candelaria turned to answer him. "Yes?" she asked.

He said to her something only they knew about. "You know, I would have married her."

Candelaria smiled and replied, "I know, Tucker. I know you would have."

They parted company and, on his way home, Tucker remembered something else he was going to give Candelaria. It was her Uncle Herman Mendoza's old portable typewriter he found stored at the newspaper office. It was lightweight, came in its own carrying case, and was still in perfectly good condition. He went back to get it and, afterward, walked to her house to leave it there for her, with a note telling her all about it.

Candelaria was already inside her house, sitting at the kitchen table. She was writing in her notebook about the sign, "Welcome to The Way," and the extraordinary sunset she had witnessed. She wondered if she was meant to see it with Tucker. Something about that place meant more to her than mere function, or even as a part of her family memories. It was a kind of power, she believed, something she wanted to understand. She always went back to it, like it was her home.

Home, to her, was a place she could never leave, only something toward which she would return. It was spiritual, she realized, and began writing a poem she entitled, "A Place Called The Way."

"It is at the center," she wrote, "a juncture of worlds, a crucible for our struggles, the Way inviting us all to step in and join the dance of spirit and of wonder, where our dreams are born and where they go to be transformed. The Way is not a word or a place in time, but a feeling, a knowing, a place outside of Time, where Truth awaits, where the life of our destined hopes invites us and brings us to our knees. The Way is not a town that became Pine Way or even Edenville. The Way is what connects us all, one heart, one soul, one life, all One."

She closed her notebook and thought about what she wrote. It brought her peace. She knew she had finally let go of her son. No more would she worry about him. He had gone home to that place from where she always knew he had originated when he was born, not from ashes and dust as in a fire or the dirt, but from the heavens, from out of the ashes of transformation and the dust of comets and stars.

Walking back to his house, Tucker stopped to see the barn once more before going home. The old structure was part of their lives. It was unimaginable it could ever be torn down. He knew how important it was to preserve Pine Way, especially the barn, and vowed to do so. He recalled his morning spent with Walter Henry, putting the sign back in its place and watching the old man carry out the ceremony. The feeling he had experienced then, returned to him. He knew it was a realization of something. It baffled him. Laughing, he slapped the air to send away his new obsession. Instead, he marveled at the mystery he could never know, yet witness continuously at the same time.

With Freckles by his side, he walked home. A light breeze, the song of crickets, and stars becoming visible high above, made tangible for him the unseen aspects of life. He pondered the many unanswered questions he had regarding that day, but let them go, preferring to savor the wisdom that dwelled within himself, simply knowing Truth, simply living. The town, the people and its history celebrated in their centennial, he knew had become part of Walter Henry's story. It was endless. Eventually, like all good stories, he mused, once the last page is read, the book must be closed. Like all special places one loves to visit, to sit and contemplate, and all sunsets gazed upon until the dusk brings down evening's curtain, one must arise and go home. He knew this to be true.

"We must take our leave," he whispered. Stepping onto his porch, he turned to look once more into the night and said, "Eventually, we all must say our last goodbyes."

EPILOGUE

Berto Mendoza sat before his rustic miner's shack, cup of coffee in hand. He was devising a scheme on how to catch his milk cow. She strayed into the woods again. Not the jefe del rancho he had envisioned himself becoming when he was a boy, but he was nevertheless happy with his life. He wrote long-winded letters to family back home in Mexico, unsure if they would ever reach their destination. He took his time writing them, oftentimes fashioning bits of poetry within their pages. So, besides being a lover, Berto Mendoza was a poet. Catching the milk cow was not in his interest, but, if he wanted cream in his coffee that morning, it was a necessity.

At the post office a while back, a bit belated for a birthday present, two or three weeks, perhaps, a small parcel arrived containing the journal in which he was writing. Along with the journal was a letter from one of his sons, Herman, who had gone to live with his sister's family in Juarez. Herman's letter was full of news about the troubles in Mexico.

A young Father Jovial, the new Catholic priest sent their way, had recently suggested holding an annual picnic in Pine Way. The same morning Berto Mendoza sat on his steps contemplating cattle rustling, Pine Way's citizens were gathering for the First Annual Pine Way Settler's Day Picnic. Picnickers arrived from all over the valley. Sounds of boisterous activity emanated from below his cabin as wagons and carriages drove past on Pine Way Junction.

His eldest son, Jesse, came walking up the road with the cow, a lead rope around her neck, cowbell clanging, and Berto was happy. At last, he could have cream in his coffee.

He called out to Lucy. "Choo-cha!" he said. "The cow! She needs to be milked." He winked at his son.

"Papá. Gorda here wasn't that hard to catch," said Jesse. "Look at her! She's practically begging to be milked!" His father's laughter always, and Jesse could not help but laugh as well. "Ay, Papá, what are we to do with you?" he asked.

Jesse enjoyed their playful exchange, but needed to leave right away for the picnic. He said his goodbyes and see-you-laters and walked back down their road to where he left the wagon when he had spotted the cow.

The day was extra-special, for he and his bride were to make their first public appearance as husband and wife. They planned to make their formal announcement at the picnic. He climbed aboard the wagon and drove it into Pine Way to pick up his bride at the way station where she would soon work no more, he promised. He also promised her that, after they furnished the house and started their family, they would bring her mother to live with them. Their life would be so happy, so beautiful, they agreed.

Approaching the way station, Jesse could see his precious Ev standing on the porch holding her white parasol. An anxious, but hopeful smile was on her face. She was wearing the white dress in which she was married. She made it herself, using a light, gossamer-like fabric, accented with needle-worked rosettes. Her dark hair was worn up and she had on the high-button shoes in fashion. She had pinned a small posy of violets to her dress. Jesse recalled their last conversation. He had consulted with her about sporting a beard and mustache, but she said, "No! Definitely not!"

They rode from there to a grove of pines where the picnic was being held. Their new house was built on the edge of that grove. Jesse could hardly wait for Ev to see their new home.

Arriving at the picnic, everyone was delighted to see them. Even though their plan to formally announce their marriage was a secret, Ev's mother told. Word spread, so everyone came prepared to celebrate. A cake, frosted and decorated, was on a table covered with a white tablecloth, and there was fruit punch in the punch bowl. Well-received hugs and kisses and congratulations met the stunned couple who, surprised and smiling, thanked everyone for their kindness.

Meanwhile, two people not attending the picnic were the orphaned brother and sister, twelve-year-old Walter Henry and his twenty-six-year-old sister, Lulabelle. No one knew she had also witnessed the murder of their father, so they never connected her nighttime screams that woke everyone in the way station to that awful incident.

Hector Shoseegan had, too late, because he was on his horse and riding off in a hurry, not long after shooting Josiah Hart. He saw her, the timid, mousey young woman peering from out of the shadows of the roadside trees. The look in her eyes he never forgot, still and blank. He wondered where her human soul had gone.

Weeks and months passed since the shootings. She became like a wild animal. Sometimes caught peering out of the woods, she resembled a creature of nature, hair uncombed, flour sack dress gray with filth, and crusts of dirt on her neck, arms, and legs. The young woman was more the size of a young girl and had turned feral.

Her mother never recovered from the loss of Henry Henry. She took to her bed and died, giving up on life and wanting only to be with her husband. Walter Henry busied himself working with Timothy Hart in the blacksmith shop and livery stable. Timothy's wife, Alice, and Harry Stewart's wife, Phoebe, took over the way station, but no one took the time to help Lulabelle. She would hide and scurry out of sight when someone saw her. When hungry, she would grab some food, then dodge into the woods to eat it.

Someone reported seeing her sitting on the pine needles beneath the forest trees, talking to a fox and a squirrel, with a jay bird on her shoulder. She was sharing her food with them, barefooted and dirty. People in town decided it was time to bring her in before winter came, or she would surely die. Using a bit of trickery, they caught her. She fought and scratched and howled and screeched, but then became absolutely docile when Walter Henry told her they were only trying to help. They brought her to a place that was newly built at the north end of the valley, called Mountain's Rest. It was a mountain get-away for city people, intended to provide a respite from the noise and ills of city living. It would one day be enlarged and renamed Spring Hill Residence & Infirmary, initially serving tuberculosis patients.

Lulabelle stayed there for a time. They cleaned her up, cut her hair, and attempted to bring civilization back to her wild, wounded heart. However, her nighttime screaming upset everyone. Phoebe Stewart and Alice Hart, who saw to Lulabelle's care, were informed she had to go. Not only was she disruptive of the quiet atmosphere, she would continually sneak wild things into her room, baby raccoons, wounded birds, and lizards, so that was that. Out of ideas, Phoebe and Alice sought the help of Lucy Shoseegan, whom everyone knew from local gossip, was a medicine woman, a healer of all sorts of maladies.

The day of the picnic, the Hart's left Lulabelle and Walter Henry at the bottom of Berto and Lucy's road. The two orphans walked up the road together and, once they arrived at the mining shack, Lulabelle's demeanor shifted away from the wild fear locked within her eyes to one of peace and calm.

Lucy approached them after closing the gate to an outbuilding and corral that housed the milk cow. Berto looked on before returning to his birthday journal and sipping his coffee. Speaking in English, Lucy invited Walter Henry to join her and Lulabelle as they followed a path into the woods toward a rocky knoll. She motioned to them to sit.

"Tell me, Walter," she said. "What happened that day? Tell me everything."

Lucy sat beside Lulabelle, quietly singing as Walter Henry began to tell his story for the very first time. It was about something that took place only the year before when he was eleven. Lulabelle was twenty-five, although she looked like a young teenager and behaved more like a little girl at times.

Lulabelle, the woman with wispy, light-brown hair that fell to her shoulders, who had been developing in the shadows, emerged from her hiding place within, as though for the first time. The breezes flowed through, stirring her hair, gently lifting the boughs of fir and pine and rustling the leaves of maple and oak. The grasses and sage flowed with it, the sound like a hushed whistling and a whirring.

According to Walter Henry, on the day of their father's murder, Lulabelle was sitting on the back porch of the way station, not wanting to help in the kitchen. She had taken to her wild ways in the woods when only a young girl and could hardly bear being indoors. An argument between their father and Josiah Hart was becoming heated, voices raised to a shout. Frightened, Lulabelle dashed toward the back door of the barn, following her brother on his way to do his chores.

Wondering when his father was coming into the barn, Walter Henry became worried about what was taking place out in the road. He went out the front door of the barn to see that his father was still arguing with Josiah. They were yelling angrily at one another and had attracted an audience, townspeople watching from shop windows and peeking from around the corners of buildings.

Lulabelle ran to her brother's side. But, when the first shot rang out, she bolted, running like a deer across the road. Walter Henry had tried to hold on to her, but everything had happened so fast. She was hiding in the trees and bushes when the second shot was fired.

Walter Henry recalled more about that day. "I saw my mother run out of the house and down the steps. I never saw her move so fast. I thought she'd surely fall. She went straight to my papa's side as he lay there in the road, blood coming out of him like he had sprung a leak. I tried to run to her, but Hector held me close to him and was singing a song I still remember. I asked him about it. He said it was the death song. I started crying, because I knew he meant that my papa was dead. I felt like I was going off to some other world, being carried away to that death place where I didn't want to go."

He paused in his storytelling, tears glistening in the sun's light. His dried cornstalk-colored hair was tousled by the wind that carried the two songs upon them. The one song was of death, to bring peace to those who had died that day and, the other, Lucy sang to call back the souls of those who yet lived, Walter Henry and his sister, Lulabelle.

Continuing his story, he said, "My mother screamed. It was an awful sound, like she was in a lot of pain, like it was the scariest thing ever." He was describing what happened to his mother as part of her departed from life while, what was left, vowed to the heavens, "I *curse* the day you were born, Josiah Hart! I pray your family knows the pain my family has suffered here today!"

Lucy sang louder, more intensely at these words. She had a bundle of sage burning and a large feather, sweeping its smoke upon Walter Henry and his sister. He sat with eyes closed and saw within himself a large bird coming at him, wings flapping and striking him with its healing power. He never asked what Lucy Shoseegan had done, what her part was, but then everything quieted, like he had returned to the present.

Leaving Lulabelle sitting on one of the boulders, Lucy led Walter Henry back down the path. She handed him the sage bundle and instructed him on what he and Lulabelle needed to do next, stressing its importance. She also told him that they were welcome to live with her and Berto.

Walter Henry thanked them both and turned to walk down the mountain to go to work at the blacksmith shop and livery stable. Before the mining shack was out of view, he looked back, wondering what his sister was doing, hoping she would be all right. What he saw he would remember all his life. At the edge of the mountain, stood the humble mining shack, smoke drifting from the campfire before it. Further up the hill, he saw tall trees, immense pine, cedar, and fir, rising upward into the bluest of skies. Lulabelle was standing away in the trees with Lucy, tiny figures all in white with the whitest of hair. Walter Henry cried in a terrible kind of joy at what his eyes beheld.

The laughter of children and the jubilant glee of men and women could be heard coming from the picnic grounds as he continued walking down the mountainside. He reached Pine Way Junction, greeted by neighbors working in their yards or seated on their porches as he happily made his way toward the barn. Sunlight filtered through the trees, brightening the leaves of willow and cottonwood along the creek, shimmering upon fields of greenery and apple blossoms in the long orchard rows. It bathed every living thing in a glorious, radiant warmth.

On that spring day, as white clouds passed swiftly along in the wind, life carried on, it continued on. When Walter Henry reached the barn, whistling "Nearer My God To Thee," Berto Mendoza sat cross-legged on his overlooking stone above the valley, contemplating how to walk the Way.

THE END

ABOUT THE AUTHOR

Corrine Ardoin has lived in California all her life. Her writing expresses her love of nature, music, animals, gardening, and family history. Her first book, *A Natural History of the Nipomo Mesa Region*, established her as a local naturalist and author. In addition to her college education, her personal interest in healing led her to later become a master-level healer using energy medicine as taught by the Four Winds Society. Her latest projects have included writing the Pine Valley series with *Fathers of Edenville*, *Mothers of Pine Way*, and *A Place Called The Way* leading into additional books in the series. Currently, she lives on the Central Coast of California with her husband.

NOTE FROM THE AUTHOR

Word-of-mouth is crucial for any author to succeed. If you
enjoyed *A Place Called The Way*, please leave a review online—
anywhere you are able. Even if it's just a sentence or two. It
would make all the difference and would be very much
appreciated.

Thanks!
Corrine Ardoin

We hope you enjoyed reading this title from: